The most famous creation in
science fiction comes to li

ADAM

The first of th   ience fiction,
and the model for   owed, Adam Link—
Robot re-appears   a novelized version of
his exciting adventures written by his creator,
Eando Binder.

Have I a soul?

Am I a menace to civilization? Should I seek
voluntary extinction?

Am I a monster—or a man?

These are but a few of the life-and-death questions Adam Link—Robot must answer. How he
copes with crisis after crisis in his amazing "life"
will provide hours of thrills and entertainment for
s-f fans old and new.

ADAM LINK — ROBOT

Eando Binder

PAPERBACK LIBRARY, Inc.

New York

PAPERBACK LIBRARY EDITION

First Printing: September, 1965

Copyright © 1965 by Paperback Library, Inc.

TABLE OF CONTENTS

CHAPTER 1

My Creation

I will begin at the beginning. I was born, or created, five years ago. I am a true robot. Some of you humans still have doubts, it seems. I am made of wires and wheels, not flesh and blood. I am run by electrical power. My brain is made of iridium-sponge.

My first recollection of consciousness was a feeling of being chained. And I was. For three days, I had been seeing and hearing, but all in a jumble. Now, I had the urge to rise and peer more closely at the strange moving form that I had seen so many times before me, making sounds.

The moving form was Dr. Charles Link, my creator. Of all the objects within my sight he was the only thing that moved. He and one other object, his dog, Terry. Even though I had not yet learned to associate movement with life, my attention was pinpointed on these two.

And on this fourth day of my life, I wanted to approach the two moving shapes and make noises at them. Particularly at the smaller one. His noises were challenging, stirring. They made me want to rise and quiet them. But I was chained. I was held down by them so that in my blank state of mind, I wouldn't wander off and bring myself to an untimely end or harm someone unknowingly.

These things, of course, Dr. Link explained to me later, when I could dissociate my thoughts and understand. I was just like a baby for those three days—a human baby. I am not as other so-called robots were—mere automatized machines designed to obey certain commands or arranged stimuli.

No, I was equipped with a pseudo-brain that could receive *all* stimuli that human brains could. And with possibilities of eventually learning to rationalize for itself.

But for three days Dr. Link was very anxious about my brain. I was like a human baby and yet I was also like a sensitive but unorganized machine, subject to the whim of mechanical chance. My eyes turned when a bit of paper fluttered to the floor. But photo-electric cells had been made previously which were capable of doing the same. My mechanical ears turned to

7

best receive sounds from a certain direction, but any scientist could duplicate that trick with sonic-relays.

The question was—did my brain, to which the eyes and ears were connected, hold on to these various impressions for future use? Did I have, in short—*memory?*

Three days I was like a newborn baby. And Dr. Link was like a worried father, wondering if his child had been born a hopeless idiot. But on the fourth day, he feared I was a wild animal. I began to make rasping sounds with my vocal apparatus, in answer to the sharp little noises the dog Terry made. I shook my swivel head at the same time, and strained against my bonds.

For a while, as Dr. Link told me, he was frightened of me. I seemed like an enraged jungle creature, ready to go berserk. He almost wanted to destroy me on the spot.

But one thing changed his mind and saved me.

The little animal Terry, barking angrily, rushed forward suddenly. It probably wanted to bite me. Dr. Link tried to call it back, but too late. Finding my smooth metal legs adamant, the dog leaped with foolish bravery in my lap, to come at my throat. One of my hands grasped it by the middle, held it up. My metal fingers squeezed too hard and the dog gave out a pained squeal.

Instantaneously, my hand opened to let the creature escape! Instantaneously. My brain had interpreted the sound for what it was. A long chain of memory-association had worked. Three days before, when I had first been brought to life, Dr. Link had stepped on Terry's foot accidentally. The dog had squealed its pain. I had seen Dr. Link, at risk of losing his balance, instantly jerk up his foot. Terry had stopped squealing.

Terry squealed when my hand tightened. He would stop when it loosened. Memory-association. The thing psychologists call reflexive reaction. A sign of a living brain.

Dr. Link tells me he let out a cry of pure triumph. He knew at a stroke I had memory. He knew I was not a wanton monster. He knew I had a thinking organ, and a first-class one. Why? Because I had reacted *instantaneously*. You will realize what that means later.

I learned to walk in three hours.

Dr. Link was still taking somewhat of a chance, unbinding my chains. He had no assurance that I would not just blunder away like a witless machine. But he knew he had to teach me to walk before I could learn to talk. The same as he knew he must bring my brain alive, fully connected to the appendages and pseudo-organs it was later to use.

If he had simply disconnected my legs and arms for those first three days, my awakening brain would never have been

8

able to use them when connected later. Do you think, if you were suddenly endowed with a third arm, that you could ever use it? Why does it take a cured paralytic so long to regain the use of his natural limbs? Mental blind spots in the brain. Dr. Link had all those strange psychological twists figured out.

Walk first. Talk and think next. That is the tried-and-true rule used among humans since the dawn of their species. Human babies learn best and most quickly that way. And I was a human baby in mind, if not body.

Dr. Link held his breath when I first tried to rise. I did, slowly, swaying on my metal legs. Up in my head, I had a three-directional spirit-level electrically contacting my brain. It told me automatically what was horizontal, vertical and oblique. My first tentative step, however, wasn't a success. My knee-joints flexed in reverse order. I clattered to my knees, which fortunately were knobbed with thick protective plates so that the more delicate swiveling mechanisms behind weren't harmed.

Dr. Link says I looked up at him like a startled child might. Then I promptly began walking along on my knees, finding this easy. Children would do this too, but it hurts them. I know no hurt.

After I had roved up and down the aisles of his workshop for an hour, chipping his furniture terribly, walking on my knees seemed completely natural. Dr. Link was in a quandary how to get me up to my full height. He tried grasping my arm and pulling me up, but my 5 0 pounds were too much for him.

My own rapidly increasing curiosity solved the problem. Like a child discovering the thrill of added height with stilts, my next attempt to rise to my full height pleased me. I tried staying up. I finally mastered the technique of alternate use of limbs and shift of weight forward.

In a couple of hours Dr. Link was leading me up and down the gravel walk around his laboratory. On my legs, it was quite easy for him to pull me along and thus guide me. Little Terry gamboled along at our heels, barking joyfully. The dog had accepted me as a friend.

I was by this time quite docile to Dr. Link's guidance. My impressionable mind had quietly accepted him as a necessary rein and check. I did, he told me later, make tentative movements in odd directions off the path, motivated by vague stimuli, but his firm arm pulling me back served instantly to keep me in line. He paraded up and down with me as one might with an irresponsible oaf.

I would have kept on walking tirelessly for hours, but Dr. Link's age quickly fatigued him and he led me inside. When he had safely gotten me seated in my metal chair, he clicked

9

the switch on my chest that broke the electric current giving me life. And for the fourth time I knew that dreamless nonbeing which corresponded to my creator's periods of sleep.

In three days I learned to talk reasonably well.

I give Dr. Link as much credit as myself. In those three days he pointed out the names of all objects in and around the laboratory. This fund of two hundred or so nouns he supplemented with as many verbs of action as he could demonstrate. Once heard and learned, a word never again was forgotten or obscured to me. Instantaneous comprehension. Photographic memory. Those things I had.

It is difficult to explain. Machinery is precise, unvarying. I am a machine. Electrons perform their tasks instantaneously. Electrons motivate my metallic brain.

Thus, with the intelligence of a child of five at the end of those three days, Dr. Link taught me to read. My photo-electric eyes instantly grasped the connection between speech and letter, as my mentor pointed them out. Thought-association filled in the gaps of understanding. I perceived without delay that the word "lion," for instance, pronounced in its peculiar way, represented a live animal crudely pictured in the book. I have never seen a lion. But I would know one the instant I did.

From primers and first-readers I graduated in less than a week to adult books. Dr. Link laid out an extensive reading course for me in his large library. It included fiction as well as factual matter. Into my receptive, retentive brain began to be poured a fund of information and knowledge never before equalled in that short period of time.

There are other things to consider besides my "birth" and "education". First of all, the housekeeper. She came in once a week to clean up the house for Dr. Link. He was a recluse, lived by himself, cooked for himself. Retired on an annuity from an invention years before.

The housekeeper had seen me in the process of construction in the past years, but only as an inanimate caricature of a human body. Dr. Link should have known better. When the first Saturday of my life came around, he forgot it was the day she came. He was absorbedly pointing out to me that "to run" meant to go faster than "to walk".

"Demonstrate," Dr. Link asked as I claimed understanding.

Obediently, I took a few slow steps before him. "Walking," I said. Then I retreated a ways and lumbered forward again, running for a few steps. The stone floor clattered under my metallic feet.

"Was—that—right?" I asked in my rather stentorian voice.

At that moment a terrified shriek sounded from the doorway. The housekeeper had come up just in time to see me perform.

She screamed, making more noise than even I. "It's the Devil himself! Run, Dr. Link—run! Police—help . . ."

She fainted dead away. He revived her and talked soothingly to her, trying to explain what I was, but he had to get a new housekeeper. After this he contrived to remember when Saturday came and on that day kept me hidden in a storeroom reading books.

A trivial incident in itself, perhaps, but very significant, as you who read this will agree.

Two months after my awakening to life, Dr. Link one day spoke to me in a fashion other than as teacher to pupil; spoke to me as man to—man.

"You are the result of twenty years of effort," he said, "and my success amazes even me. You are little short of being a human in mind. You are a monster, a creation, but you are basically human. You have no heredity. Your environment is molding you. You are the proof that mind is an electrical phenomenon, molded by environment. In human beings, their bodies—called heredity—are environment. But out of you I will make a mental wonder!"

His eyes seemed to burn with a strange fire, but this softened as he went on.

"I knew I had something unprecedented and vital twenty years ago when I perfected an iridium-sponge sensitive to the impact of a single electron. It was the sensitivity of thought! Mental currents in the human brain are of this micro-magnitude. I had the means now of duplicating mind-currents in an artificial medium. From that day to this I worked on the problem.

"It was not long ago that I completed your 'brain'—an intricate complex of iridium-sponge cells. Before I brought it to life, I had your body built by skilled artisans. I wanted you to begin life equipped to live as closely to the human way as possible. How eagerly I awaited your debut into the world!"

His eyes shone.

"You surpassed my expectations. You are not merely a thinking robot. A metal man. You are—*life!* A new kind of life. You can be trained to think, to reason, to perform. In the future, your kind can be of inestimable aid to man and his civilization. You are the first of your kind."

11

CHAPTER 2

Frankenstein!

The days and weeks slipped by. My mind matured and gathered knowledge steadily from Dr. Link's library. I was able, in time, to absorb a page of reading matter, as quickly as human eyes scan lines. You know of the television princple— a pencil of light moving hundreds of times a second over the object to be transmitted. My eyes, triggered with speedy electrons, could do the same. What I read was absorbed—memorized—instantly. From then on it was part of my knowledge.

Scientific subjects particularly claimed my attention. There was always something indefinable about human things, something I could not quite grasp, but in my science-compounded brain science digested easily. It was not long before I knew all about myself and why I "ticked" much more fully than most humans know why they live, think and move.

Mechanical principles became starkly simple to me. I made suggestions for improvementes in my own make-up that Dr. Link readily agreed upon correcting. We added little universals in my fingers, for example, that made them almost as supple as their human models.

Almost, I say. The human body is a marvelously perfected organic machine. No robot will ever equal it in sheer efficiency and adaptability. I realized my limitations.

Perhaps you will realize what I mean when I say that my eyes cannot see all colors, just the three primary hues—red, yellow and blue. It would take an impossibly complex series of units, bigger than my whole body, to enable me to see all colors. Nature has packed all that in two globes the size of marbles, for *her* robots. She had a billion years to do it. Dr. Link only had twenty years.

But my brain, that was another matter. Equipped with only two senses of three-color sight and limited sound, it was yet capable of garnishing a full experience. Smell and taste are gastronomic senses. I do not need them. Feeling is a device of Nature's to protect a fragile body. My body is not fragile.

Sight and sound are the only two cerebral senses. Einstein, color-blind, half-deaf, and with deadened senses of taste, smell and feeling, would still have been Einstein mentally.

Those were the facts. I turned the angle-iron back myself. Blood streaked my fingers when I raised his head, not knowing for the moment that he was surely dead.

But of course, I was taken for his *murderer*.

The housekeeper had also heard the noise and came from the house to investigate. She took one look. She saw me bending over the body, its head torn and bloody. She fled, too frightened to make a sound.

I am not sure what your emotion of sorrow is. Perhaps I cannot feel that deeply. But I do know that the sunlight seemed suddenly faded to me.

My thoughts are rapid. I stood there only a minute, but in that time I made up my mind to leave. This again was misinterpreted. It was considered an admission of guilt. The criminal escaping from the scene of his crime. I did not realize the web I was weaving around myself.

My abrupt departure was just a desire and determination to carry out Dr. Link's plans for me. To go out in the world and find my place in it.

To become a citizen!

Dr. Link, and my life with him, was a closed book. No use now to stay and watch ceremonials. He had launched my life. He was gone. My place now must be somewhere out in a world I had never seen. No thought entered my mind of what you humans would decide about me. I thought all men were like Dr. Link, kind and wise.

I took a fresh battery, repla'ing my half-depleted one. I would need another in 48 hours, but I was sure this would be taken care of by anyone to whom I made the request.

I left. Terry followed me. He was with me all the time in the events that followed. I have heard a dog is man's best friend. Even a metal man's.

My conceptions of geography soon proved hazy. I had pictured earth as teeming with humans and cities, leaving not much space in between. I had estimated that the city Dr. Link had spoken of must be just over the hill from his secluded country home. Yet the woods I traversed seemed endless.

Night came. I had to stop and stay still in the dark. I leaned against a tree motionlessly. Terry curled at my feet and slept. The hours passed slowly. I do not "sleep".

"Adam Link, American citizen!" I thought to myself, wondering when that day would come.

Then at dawn they appeared—the mob. Men armed with clubs, scythes and guns. They spied me and garbled shouts went up. "Dr. Link's robot!—the monster!—killer!" Then something struck my frontal plate with a clang. A bullet.

15

"Stop—wait!" I shouted, bewildered. Why was I being hunted like a wild beast? I had taken a step forward, hand upraised. But they would not listen, or explain. More shots rang out, denting my metal body. I turned and ran. Bullets might harm me, in time, if they shattered my eyes or other delicate mechanisms. Terry followed me faithfully, barking back at them.

My thoughts were puzzled. Here was something I could not rationalize or understand. This was so different from the world I had learned about in books. What had happened to the sane and orderly world my mind had conjured for itself? What was wrong?

All that day it was the same, as I ran. The party, swelled by added recruits, split into groups that tried to ring me in. They tracked me by my heavy footprints. My speed saved me each time. Yet some of those bullets damaged me. One struck the joint of my right knee, so that my leg twisted as I ran. One smashed into my head and shattered the right tympanum, making me deaf on that side.

But the bullet that hurt me most was the one that killed Terry. The posse had shot my little friend accidentally.

I was hopelessly lost now. I went in circles through the endless woods. At dusk I saw something familiar—Dr. Link's laboratory. Blindly, numbly, I crept in. It was deserted. Dr. Link's body was gone.

My birthplace! My six months of life here whirled through my mind. I felt sad. My two friends were gone, Dr. Link, and Terry. The shadows around me seemed to dance like little Terry had danced.

Then I found the book—*Frankenstein*—lying on the desk whose drawers had been emptied untidily. Dr. Link's private desk. He had kept this one book from me. Why? I read it now, in a half hour, by my page-at-a-time scanning.

And then I understood. They thought I had "turned Frankenstein" and had killed Dr. Link, my creator. They had only one thought in mind, that I was a created monster of metal who had gone "berserk", lacking a soul.

Adam Link, American citizen? No, it was Adam Link, Frankenstein monster.

That, I saw, was my epitaph.

Soon it was close to dawn. I knew there was no hope for me. They had me surrounded, cut off. I had not been so badly damaged that I could not still summon power enough to run through their lines and escape. But it would only be at the cost of several of their lives. And that was the reason I stayed my hand against them, as the yelling mob stormed in.

16

Clubs and guns were raised against me. Hate was in their faces. I closed my eyes, to shut out the sight. It was the end, my thoughts said, of Adam Link, the first of intelligent robots —and the last.

CHAPTER 3

My Arrest

I opened my eyes, astonished, a moment later. I looked around and saw the group of men who had hunted me down. But they had stopped. Why hadn't they smashed and pounded me to broken wheels and scattered mechanical parts?

Then I saw the blazing-eyed young man facing them. The armed party was muttering and waving their weapons at me, but my unexpected champion had evidently halted them.

He turned to me now. He was young, firm-jawed, and vaguely familiar in some way. He had grey intelligent eyes. I liked him instantly. Though I am a robot, I form likes and dislikes among the humans I meet.

"Are you all right—Adam Link?" he asked. He added the name given me by Dr. Link with some hesitation, but clearly. He was addressing me as one living entity to another. To use a more appropriate expression—as man to man. Only one other had ever done that—Dr. Link.

I arose from my sitting posture, in which I had been since I had turned myself off. I nearly toppled over. One of my legs was badly twisted. I took swift appraisal and noticed the dents on my metal-wrought shoulders and chest. The top of my skull-plate too, was dented, pressing down slightly on the electrical brain within. From that, for lack of a better term, I had a headache.

Obviously, I had been saved just in time. The enraged, vengeful posse had begun to smash me. But no vital harm had been done.

"I can be repaired," I replied. The armed men fell back uneasily at the sound of my microphonic voice. Why are humans so afraid of that which they cannot understand? Then I looked at the young man, wishing I could show gratitude.

"Thank you for what you have done," I said. "Who are you?"

"I'm Thomas Link, Dr. Link's nephew, and his closest living relative," he said. Instantly I saw the family resemblance, and knew why he had seemed so familiar, though I had never seen him before.

He went on, speaking to the others as much as myself. "I

18

have been practicing law, in San Francisco. I hurried here when I heard of my uncle's death. He has left everything to me. I see I have come just in time to prevent the destruction— the wanton *murder*, gentlemen—of Adam Link, my uncle's intelligent robot."

"Huh—murder," said the leader of the men, scoffingly. He was the county sheriff and carried a high-powered rifle under his arm. "This—this *thing* isn't a man. It's a machine. A clever diabolical machine that killed your uncle in cold blood."

"I don't believe it," snapped young Tom Link quickly. "My uncle wrote me many letters about this robot. He said it was as rational as any human being. Perhaps more so than you, sheriff. And not in the least dangerous, in any remote Frankenstein way. My uncle was a clear-headed thinker and scientist. What he said, I accept. You will not destroy this robot."

The sheriff's face reddened. Tom had been rather tactless in comparing him and myself. "We will!" he shouted. "It's a dangerous monster. As the representative of the law in this matter, it is my rightful duty to protect the community. If a tiger were loose in this county, I would destroy it." He raised his rifle and the men behind him muttered with rising feelings.

I wonder if I have an emotion akin to your human anger? He had compared me to a tiger! I know what a tiger is, from my extensive reading. My electronic brain hummed, and I started to speak, but Tom Link motioned me silent.

"Stop, sheriff," he said warningly. "The robot—if you choose to consider it that way—was part of my uncle's *property*. Now it is *my* property. I am a lawyer. I know my rights. If you touch the robot, I'll sue you in court for willful destruction of a piece of my property."

The law officer gasped. "Well—uh—" He began again, lamely. "But this is different. This robot is a moving, li—no, not living—but anyway—uh—it's a creature, and—" He was too muddled by the sudden change of concept to go on.

Tom Link smiled. I suddenly perceived that he was a very clever young man. He had planned this *trap*. "Right, sheriff," he said quickly. "This robot is a creature. It is not an animal, for animals don't talk. It is a manlike being. Therefore, like any other talking, thinking man, *he is entitled to a court trial*."

The sheriff tried to remonstrate, but Tom hustled him out, and the other men with him. "If you want to continue prosecution of Adam Link, the intelligent robot," was Tom's parting shot, "come back with a warrant of arrest."

Tom turned to me when we were alone. "Whew!" He wiped his forehead. "That was close." Then he grinned a little, thinking perhaps of the utterly confounded look on the

19

sheriff's face. I grinned, too, within myself. It is a feature of intelligence—whether in a human body or metal—to see humor in that which is ridiculous.

I was still, however, a little puzzled. "Tell me, Tom Link," I queried, "why you have so completely taken my side? All others, except your uncle, hated and feared me from first sight."

Instead of answering, Tom rummaged in his uncle's private desk. At last he withdrew a document and let me read it. I did not quite grasp the complicated legal language, but I noticed the word "citizen" several times.

Tom explained. "My uncle, if he hadn't died so unfortunately, was fully determined to make you a *citizen,* Adam Link, as you know. He had begun to take up the matters of legal records to prove your 'birth', education and rightful status. He corresponded with me on these details at some length. In another month, I was to have come here to complete the negotiations."

I remembered Dr. Link's repeated remarks that I was not just a robot, a metal man. I was *life!* I was a thinking being, as manlike as any clothed in flesh and blood. He had trained me, brought me up, with all the loving kindness, patience and true feeling of a father with his own child.

And now, with the thought of my creator, came a sadness, an ache within me. I felt as I had that day I discovered him dead, when the sunlight had seemed suddenly faded to me. You who read may smile cynically, but my "emotions", I believe, are real and deep. Life is essentially in the mind. I have a mind.

"He was a good man," I said. "And you, Tom, you are my friend."

He smiled in his warm way, and put his hand on my shiny, hard shoulder. "I am your *cousin,*" he responded simply, "Blood is thicker than water, you know."

No play of words was intended, I knew that. I can only say that I have never heard a nobler expression. In simple words, he showed me that he accepted me as a fellow man.

The rest of that day, Tom Link went through his uncle's effects while he talked to me. I told him the full story of his uncle's accidental death and the following events.

"We have a battle ahead of us," he summed it up. "The battle to save you from a charge of manslaughter. After that, we will take up the matter of your—citizenship."

He glanced at me just a little queerly. His eyes traveled from my mirrored eyes and expressionless metal face down to my stiff alloy legs. Perhaps for the first time, it occurred to him how strange this all was. He, a young lawyer, out to defend me, a conglomerate of wires and cogs, as though I were a human being, conceived by woman. For a moment, he may even have had doubts, now that the excitement was over and he had a chance to think about me.

Might I not be a monster after all? Might Dr. Link not have been wrong in saying that I was the *opposite* of my fearsomely fabricated exterior? Who could know what weird thoughts coursed through my unhuman, unbiological brain? Might I not just be waiting for the chance to kill Tom, too, in some monstrous mood?

I could sense those thoughts crowding his mind. I don't think it's a telepathic phenomenon. It is just that my electron-activated brain works instantaneously. The chains of memory-association within me operate with lightning rapidity. The slightest twitch of his lip and inflection in his voice revealed to me the probable thought causing them.

I felt a little disturbed. Was my only friend to gradually turn against me? Was my cause hopeless? Was it a foregone conclusion that such an utterly alien being as myself could never be accepted in the world of man? I was like a Martian, suddenly descending upon Earth, with as little possibility of achieving friendly intercourse. You think the comparison irrelevant? I will guarantee that the first Martians, or other-world creatures, to land on Earth—if this event ever occurs—will be destroyed blindly. You humans do not know how strong and deep within you lies the jungle instincts of your animal past. That is, in the majority of you. And it is not necessarily those in high places who are more "civilized". But I digress again.

While Tom was busy, I repaired myself. I am a machine, and know more about my workings than any physiologist knows of his own body. I straightened the knee-joint swivel mechanism, twisted by a bullet. Two of my fingers had broken "muscle" cables which I welded together. I took off my frontal chest plate and hammered out the dents. My removable skull-piece allowed me to release the pressure on my sponge-brain. My "headache" left.

Finally I oiled myself completely, and substituted a fresh battery in my driving unit. In a few hours I had gone through what would correspond in a human to surgical patchings, operations and convalescence that would have taken weeks. It is very convenient having a metal body.

Then I went out. I wandered in the woods and came back with little Terry's half-decayed body. I buried him in the backyard, thinking of his joyous barks and the playful times we had had together.

"Adam! Adam Link!"

I started and turned. It was Tom behind me, watching. His face was self-reproachful.

"Forgive me," he said softly. "I was doubting you, Adam Link, all afternoon. Doubting that you could be as nearly human as my uncle wrote you were. But I will never fail you again." He was looking at Terry's fresh grave.

As Tom had predicted, Sheriff Barclay promptly appeared the next morning, with a warrant for my arrest. He was determined to have me destroyed. Since he couldn't do so directly, without legally entangling himself in a suit, he had taken the other course.

"It will be a damned farce—holding a trial for a robot," he admitted shamefacedly. "I feel like a fool. But it must be destroyed. You're rather clever, young man, but you don't think a jury of honest, level-headed men is going to exonerate your—uh—client?"

Tom said nothing, just set his jaw grimly.

Sheriff Barclay looked at me. "You're—uh—I mean *it's* under arrest. It must come with us, to jail." He was speaking to Tom, although he watched me narrowly, expecting me, I suppose, to go berserk.

"I'm coming along," nodded Tom. "Come, Adam."

They had brought a truck for me—I am a 500-pound mass of metal—and drove me toward the nearby town. I had never been in one before, having lived in seclusion with Dr. Link at his country place. My first glimpse of the small city with its 50,000 inhabitants did not startle me. It was about what I had expected from my reading and the pictures I had seen —noisy, congested, ugly, badly arranged.

A curious crowd watched as I was paraded up the courthouse steps. The news had gone around. They watched silently, awestruck. And in every face, I saw lurking fear, instinctive hatred. I had the feeling then, as never before, that I was an outcast. And doomed.

The scene in the courtroom was, as the sheriff had predicted, a sort of solemn farce. The presiding judge coughed continuously. Only Tom Link was at his ease. He insisted on the full legal method. There had been an inquest of course before Dr. Link's burial, in which it was established that a heavy instrument had caused death. Nothing could gainsay that my hard metal arm might have been the "instrument of death".

I was indicted on a manslaughter charge for the death of Dr. Charles Link, and entered in the record as "Adam Link".

When that had been done, Tom heaved a sigh and winked toward me. I knew what the wink meant. Again a trap had been laid, and sprung. Once my name was down in the court record, I was accorded all the rights and privileges of the machinery of justice. As I know now, if Sheriff Barclay had gone to the governor of the state instead, he could have obtained a state order to demolish me as an *unlawful weapon!* For I was a mechanical contrivance that (circumstantially) had taken a life.

Tom could not have squirmed out of that charge. But Sheriff Barclay had missed that loophole. With my name down, I was a defendant—and had human status.

Two newspaper reporters were present. One of them was staring at me closely, wonderingly. He came as near as he could, unafraid. Unafraid! The only one in the room, besides Tom, who did not fear me instinctively. He, too, could be my friend.

I saw the question in his eager young face. "Yes, I am intelligent," I said, achieving a hissing whisper, so no one else would hear.

He started, then grinned pleasantly. "Okay!" he said and I know he believed. He began scribbling furiously in a notebook.

The formal indictment over, the bailiff led me to my cell and locked me in. Tom smiled reassurance, but when he left, I felt suddenly alone, hemmed in by enemies. You humans can never have quite that feeling. Unless, perhaps, you are a spy caught by an enemy nation. But even then you know you are dying for a cause, a reason. But I was being doomed—*exterminated*—for little else than not being understood.

Tom appeared again an hour later, waving a paper. The court officials were with him, arguing loudly. He turned.

"Habeas Corpus!" he kept saying, calmly. "You've indicted Adam Link, whether he has the body of a robot or an elephant. This writ of Habeas Corpus frees the *person* of Adam Link, till the trial is called. I know the law. Release him."

The bailiff argued hotly. I digested what I had heard, slowly and carefully. That is, slowly for me. It wasn't more than a second later that I grasped the bars of my cell-door and with one concerted tug, jerked it open. There was a terrific grind of metal. The broken lock clattered to the stone floor. I strode out.

"I do not like being in a cage," I said. "Can we go, Tom?"

I am afraid my impulsive act was a mistake. I saw that by Tom's face. I had displayed my great strength, the strength of a powerful machine. It could only add fuel to their fear of me. The officials all turned pale and stumbled back, perhaps visioning how easy it would be for me to crush their skulls with single blows of my steel hands.

23

And that was precisely the last thing they must think of me. They must come to appreciate my mind, and my ability to serve humanity. For that purpose, Dr. Link had created me. And for that purpose I had dedicated myself, independently, months before. Once accepted as a fellow *mind*—a monster only in appearance—I could show my true worth. I, Adam Link, was the first of intelligent robots. I could serve civilization in the combined capacity of mind and machine.

Yes, it was a foolish mistake. The writ of Habeas Corpus would have freed me anyway, if I had given Tom a little time. As I realize now, I was bewildered and impatient. I cannot understand the strange tortuous ways you humans have of doing things. I have much to learn of civilization. Much.

Tom did not reprimand me, however. Grasping my hand, he led me out of the jail. The officials stared dumfoundedly. Tom had also paid bail, and procured a paper placing me in his custody.

Thereafter, in the time before the trial, I went with Tom around the city. He made frequent visits to the bank that was settling the estate of Dr. Link. He took me to the public library when he sought reference in weighty law books. Often he would just parade me down a street. We watched the reaction of the crowds narrowly. As Tom had put it—could we get public opinion to swing our way, in the coming battle for my status in human society?

Fear! It rose in overwhelming tides about me. Blind fear that sent people scurrying away without dignity. Sometimes cars, in the traffic, bumped one another as their drivers caught their first glimpse of my shiny, metal form, so manlike and yet so alien. I felt depressed. Must I always inspire fear?

Children, however, proved more quickly adaptable. They had more curiosity. In fact, a group of street gamins took to following me, tossing pebbles to hear them clink against my metal body. And a chant arose among them: "You're nothing but a tin can! You're nothing but a tin can!"

I wasn't annoyed, nor was I particularly amused. Some of the adults we passed tittered. People cannot laugh and fear at the same time. The gamins with their simple little song had proved a blessing in disguise. Even Tom—though he tried to hide it—had a lurking grin twitching at his lips. I began to have hope that the fear of me would die down, eventually.

But it was a forlorn hope. My first venture into the public library was disquieting—both to myself and others. People edged away from me hurriedly. The library officials tried to prevent my going around to seek books, but Tom calmly and stubbornly proved to them that they couldn't eject me on any

24

count short of violation of civil liberties. The librarians gave in, but summoned the police for guard. Undoubtedly everyone had heard of me as the murderer of a man. Everyone was certain that at any moment I would wantonly kill another. I felt that, and it saddened me.

But again there was an amusing quality in it. I eased my weight into a chair in the reading room and began reading scientific books Tom had procured for me at the call-desk. I scanned a page at a time.

An elderly man opposite me at the reading table had not looked up. Absorbed in his reading, he had ignored the noise I could not avoid making as my metal form contacted the chair. But in the following quiet, the steady hum of my internal mechanism must have penetrated his deep study. He looked up suddenly, flashed a glance of annoyance at me, and looked down again. Ten seconds passed before he looked up again, realizing what he had seen. This time he was startled. He closed his eyes, snapped them open again. After another long look at me, he quietly arose, as though recalling another engagement, and left. His face was pale.

The newspapers were particularly unkind to me. Daily editorials were written, denouncing the laxity of the law and police. They were allowing, it was said, a dangerous engine of destruction to walk about. I was the Frankenstein product of a mad genius, a twisted travesty of the human form. The Machine had finally arisen, as had been foretold in imaginative literature, threatening Mankind. I was the forerunner, the spy perhaps, of a secret horde of metal demons, waiting to descend crushingly upon humanity.

One editorial writer, however, denounced the denouncers. He took my part, insisting there was not a shred of proof as yet that Dr. Link's amazing robot was a menace of any kind. I know he must be the young reporter I had seen at the court. I had an unexpected friend, two now, with Tom.

Two—out of the 50,000 in that city. Or out of the millions elsewhere who had read of me and promptly were my enemies.

CHAPTER 4

People vs. Robot

There was one other thing that happened during those two weeks. The fire. Tom and I were walking down the street when we heard the shriek of sirens. Then we saw it ahead—smoke pouring from the windows of a ten-story tenement. In the excitement of that, even I became of secondary importance. People crowded at my very side, staring at the flaming building, hardly aware of me.

Suddenly, after it was thought that all had been rescued, two screaming faces appeared at the seventh story. Smoke gushed from behind them.

A hideous wail went up from the crowd. They were doomed, those two! The ladders were threatened by flame and had to be withdrawn. No fireman dared plunge into the raging inferno of the interior. Jumping nets were in readiness, but the two screaming voices choked off and the two faces vanished from the window. Smoke had suffocated them into insensibility. In a matter of seconds, their fate would be sealed. . . .

My reactions are instantaneous, being those of a machine. I moved away from Tom, toward the building. He was unaware, staring up with a look of hypnotic horror, as were all the crowd. They were in my way. I had to get through quickly.

I raised my voice in a hoarse bellow that was easily heard over the roaring of the flames. The crowd, suddenly turning its attention to me and as quickly panic-stricken in the fear that I was going berserk, melted away. I dashed into the curtain of smoke that wreathed the burning building.

Hissing flames were all about me. I dashed through them, my metal body knowing no hurt or pain, and having no lungs to be seared. But it was a task even for my sharp, mechanical vision to see the stairs through the rolling clouds of black smoke. Fortunately, the stairs were of metal. I raced up them with all the speed and power I could command from my mechanical body. I reached the seventh floor just in time. The stairs behind me collapsed, melted through. I could never go back that way.

I found the two still figures, a young man and woman, on

the floor, in their smoke-filled room. Roughly, since there wasn't much time, I threw them one over each shoulder.

If there was time!

The only way led up, to the roof. Another curtain of flame had to be traversed. Summoning all my powers, I dashed through, my metal legs pounding. The clothing of the two limp forms I carried did not catch fire. Nor, I hoped, had their skins felt more than a momentary withering blast. Yet for all I knew, they were already dead.

Escape from the roof resolved itself into one uncertain chance—leaping across to the next building. The distance, I automatically knew when I looked, was thirty feet. To make it worse, the next rampart was on a higher level. I would have to leap thirty feet across, five feet upward, carrying almost three hundred pounds—plus five hundred pounds of my own weight —of inert load. If I failed—a drop of more than a hundred feet to the hard concrete of a courtyard.

Yes, I knew fear. Or at least, something within my brain that sickened at the thought of three broken bodies, two of them human pulp, lying down there.

There was no time to waste, or think. I was alone up here, and the decision was mine to make. I took a long run, leaped —and made it.

It is simple to say it, though the bare words leave much unsaid. At the moment of leaping, I flexed my metal legs with such force that the stone eave beneath them cracked. I would have been a strange sight, I suppose, had anyone seen—a metal Tarzan flying through the air, with two limp human forms slung over its shoulders. Thirty feet across and five upward! Only the tremendous powers inherent in my motorized body made it possible. And even their limit was taxed. I landed with one foot on the other rampart and teetered for a moment, at the brink of disaster.

I had just time to shove the bodies forward onto the roof safely, as my other foot clawed vainly for purchase. At least they had been saved. Then I slipped backward and wondered how it would "feel" to smash against the hard concrete a hundred feet below. My clawing foot met something—the jutting edge of a window frame. It saved me. A moment later I was standing over the two bodies, looking back at the roof we had left. It was cracking and fingers of flame shot up from the hell below.

I picked up the two forms and clattered down this building's outside fire-escape, laying the two figures in the courtyard. They were breathing and moaning. They were alive. Their clothing was singed and blackened where it had pressed against

27

my heated metal shoulders. Some few burns and blisters were on their faces and hands. But they would survive.

I waited till my metal body had cooled completely before I left the courtyard to bring others. As soon as I stepped out into the street, people, with their nerves already tense, shrieked and ran from me. I tried to speak but no one listened.

Tom came running up. "Good God, Adam!" he panted. "Where have you been?" He grabbed my hand and pulled me toward his car, parked some blocks away. "When you bellowed and leaped away so suddenly before," he continued, "everyone thought you had gone wild. The crowd has been murmuring against you. Hurry. A mob will do anything. Hurry!"

Half the crowd had surged after us, transferring their blind, helpless rage at the fire to me. I picked up Tom in my arms and raced for our car, outstripping any pursuers. I drove the car myself, away from the threatening people and out of the city.

It was not till we had gone several miles, and no pursuit appeared, that Tom became calmer and looked at me. He looked over my body, his eyes suddenly wide and comprehending. "Adam! Those soot-streaks—you look like you'd been in the fire—?"

I told my story. Tom sat silently for a while, just staring at me. "You risked your own—life," he murmured finally. "And no one saw you do it?"

"No one," I told him.

"The irony of it," Tom said with a groan. "If there had been one witness, the story would have made you a hero. Now, you'd never be believed. The rescued pair will probably believe they escaped themselves, somehow. And I'm just afraid—" He went on frankly, his voice a little hollow. "I'm not as confident in winning for you, as I was at first. Public opinion—and that will mean the jury—is stupidly against you from the start. Adam, we may lose . . ."

The trial was the next day.

That evening, I noticed the change in my young friend. Up to this time he had been eager, jubilant, accepting the unprecedented defense of a metal intelligence as a most unique chance to match his legal wits against the ponderous machinery of law. Now he was worried, depressed, as the hour drew near.

So much has been written of the trial that I will give you only my own reactions, thoughts, observations. I was placed in custody of the court early in the morning. The first day of the trial began at noon, before a packed audience.

I, Adam Link, was the defendant. Thomas Link was my defense counselor. The prosecutor was the city's most prominent attorney, requisitioned by Sheriff Barclay in his determination

28

to rid the community of a "dangerous menace". The jurors were twelve average citizens of the city. All of them watched me continuously with eyes that held no sympathy or understanding—only hostile fear and unreasoning hatred.

In all that courtroom, only one man was on my side—Tom himself. No, two. There was also the reporter who had been my editorial champion. He sat in the press box, and waved a greeting to me, which I returned. There were several other reporters, from big cities, who obviously looked upon the whole thing as some comic-opera hoax, or gigantic publicity stunt.

Of all the human institutions with which I have come in contact, your courtroom proceedings are to me the most confusing. It seems an endless turmoil of questions, evasions and half-truths. It is like hacking one's way through the jungles I have read about, and going ever in circles.

The prosecution slowly proceeded to pin the murder of Dr. Link on me, by circumstantial evidence. To bolster his accusations, the prosecutor called me to the witness chair. The crowd sat up stiffly and the room became utterly silent. They were about to hear an allegedly intelligent creation of mineral matter talk. I suppose it is hard to believe.

"Adam Link, you are a machine? You are strong?" asked the attorney.

"Yes, to both questions," I answered.

"You could kill any human being with your metal hands?"

"Yes."

"You could, in fact, kill a dozen men with a dozen blows?"

"Yes."

The prosecutor had fired the questions like a machine-gun. I had answered quickly, as I always do. Tom looked at me helplessly, having had no chance to object. I knew what he wanted of me—evasion, hedging. But I am a machine. I have not learned to smother truth.

You can guess how the rest went. The prosecutor led me through my story of the death of my creator, with leading questions that constantly highlighted my brute power.

Tom was sweating when he questioned me. He, in turn, attempted to bring to the fore my humanlike intelligence and thoughts. He quoted from his uncle's letters concerning me. He had volunteer professors from the city's college ask me scientific questions. I rather think I amazed them, for I had read Dr. Link's extensive private library from beginning to end. My photographic memory supplied the answers to questions in biology, physics, chemistry, astronomy, and down the line. I added, multiplied, or took cube roots of any sets of complicated numbers instantly. Often they had to check for many minutes, with paper and pencil. Electrons move at the speed of light. Electrons motivate my brain.

Tom glowed with brief triumph. The air within the court had subtly changed. There was respect for me, if nothing else. The prosecutor then seized opportunity. He magnanimously admitted my intellect but—*where was my soul?*

The trial rapidly resolved itself into something a little more significant than the mere death of one man. By the second day —I spent a night in the hated jail—a stark issue arose.

Could I, an intelligent but alien being, be allowed to live and move in the world of men?

Two portions of the interminable proceedings stand clearly imprinted in my mind. First, the prosecutor's most oratorical moment, when he shouted:

"Adam Link, as we have been forced to call him, is a *thing* without a soul. Without a spark of human feeling within his cold metallic body. He can know nothing of the emotions of kindliness, sympathy, mercy. If once he is given a place in human society, he will slay and destroy. He has no right to live. No thing that mocks the human body and its divine intellect has any place in our civilization. You men of the jury, remember that your decision will set a precedent. This is a grave responsibility. Science, long prophesying it, has finally produced the intelligent robot. And look what it has immediately become—*a killer! A Frankenstein!*"

Frankenstein! Again that hideous, twisted allusion. The word alone, in the popular mind, is a misconception, for Frankenstein's monster was *driven* to his deeds.

The prosecutor pointed an accusing finger at me. All the crowd shrank a little, seeing me in the light he had conjured.

Tom's closing speech was eloquent, but futile.

"Adam Link is a human being in all but body. His body is a machine and machines serve humanity. The *mind* of Adam Link thinks the way we do, perhaps even in a superior degree. Gentlemen of the jury, if you find the defendant guilty, you are sending an innocent *man* to death."

I looked at the jury, at the audience, at the court officials. Tom was talking to a blank wall. I searched for one ray of sympathy, understanding, but found none. Yes, one—the reporter who had braved opinion before. But he was only one out of hundreds facing me. I felt at that moment a bottomless despair. I had felt that way once before—looking down at the dead body of Dr. Link and realizing I must face the future without his friendship and guidance.

The jury filed out to decide my fate.

Court was adjourned, and I was taken under guard to the jail, to await recall. The way led around the front of the courthouse, to the neighboring jail building. Something of a crowd, unable to get into the court, had collected outside. Tom walked beside me, haggard and hopeless.

Suddenly, he was whispering in my ear. "I've failed you, Adam. We've lost, I know. Adam"—he looked around—"make a break for it. Run away now. It's your best chance. Perhaps somewhere you can hide, find a way to live. Run, Adam!"

He pushed at me. I think he was nearly out of his mind, from the strain of the past few days. I gripped his shoulder and steadied him. "No, Tom," I said. "There is no place for me in your world. I will accept—"

And then I suddenly *did* leap away. I am afraid I bowled over two of the police escorting me. I had gone twenty yards before the gasp of the nearby crowd indicated that they had seen what I had seen.

I had seen and comprehended, seconds before anyone else, the tragedy impending out in the street. A little boy on roller skates had lost balance. I saw the first twist of his little body, that told me he would fall. Also the car. It was coming at a fair rate of speed down the street. Its driver was carelessly viewing the crowd on the sidewalk.

All things relating to distances, measures, and numbers integrate instantaneously in my brain, itself a mathematical instrument. I can explain it no more simply. I *knew* the boy on roller skates was going to sprawl in front of that car. I *knew* the driver, with his slow human reflexes, would perceive thi , and jam on his brakes *seconds too late*. I even knew that ne right front wheel would pass over the child's chest, and   e car would roll from 3 to 5 feet further before it stopped. The boy would be dead.

A fraction of a second to note all this. Another few seconds running, at a speed that is impossible to humans. And then I was in front of the sprawling boy, between him and the careening car. There was no time to snatch him up, with my hard metal hands, without bruising him terribly. But the car could be stopped.

I braced myself at the proper angle, right shoulder forward, crouching. There was the loud impact of metal on metal. The car's radiator struck my shoulder as I had planned. For a moment it was machine fighting machine, with a life at stake. The car, with its greater weight, pushed me back five feet—six— seven—*ten!* My feet—flat plates of tough metal—dug into the asphalt of the paving, gouging out two deep trenches.

Then the car stopped, its engine dying with a strangled gasp. My heel plates were five inches from the fallen child's body.

Close enough. I congratulated myself. I had figured it would be seven inches.

When I straightened up, my right arm dangled uselessly, as I had expected. My right shoulder plate was a crumpled mass. The heavy frontal plate of my chest bore a frayed dent five inches deep. Another half-inch would have shattered an electrical distributor within and rendered me helpless prey to the rolling car, along with the child. But I had allowed for that five-inch dent also, when fixing my body in position before the impact.

A dead silence seemed to hang over the scene as I looked around. No one moved. Hundreds of pairs of eyes stared as though in a trance. The little boy on roller skates struggled up, whimpering with fright—mostly at seeing me. Then a woman rushed to him from the crowd, taking him in her arms.

At that moment, a court official hurried from the courtroom, telling the police guard to bring back the prisoner. The jury had already made up its verdict, in a short minute.

Back in the courtroom, the foreman of the jury arose. Everyone knew what the verdict would be:

"We, the jury, find the defendant *guilty* of the murder of Dr. Link, in the first degree."

Tom looked sadly at me. A hush came over the crowd. All eyes were on me, wondering what the machine with a mind would do or say. I did and said nothing. I had told Tom I would accept my fate.

The judge pronounced sentence: Death in the electric chair, three days later. Electricity would burn out my brain, of course, as readily as that of a human being.

Later, I was locked in my cell. Heavy chains that even I could not break bound me to the wall. They were not necessary. I would not have tried to escape. I would not have wanted to live in a world that did not want me.

One thing had given me satisfaction, or else I would have contemplated passing from the scene with deep regrets. Tom visited me in my cell accompanied by a grave, distinguished man. He was one of the world's greatest legal men. Seeing the brilliance of Tom through the trial, against insuperable odds, he had offered Tom a position in his office. Thus Tom's future had not been blasted by his unselfish labors in my hopeless cause.

I must mention, too, the visit of the young reporter I have mentioned several times. I did not even know his name at the time. But he told me he was convinced that he had seen justice go wrong, once again. At the last he made a gesture I fully realized had great significance. *He shook hands with me*. Tears were foreign to me, but something blurred my vision as he strode away.

It was amusing in a way, the last thing I wrote down about my experiences. I had told them how simple it was to "execute" me. They would just have to turn off the master switch on my chest and smash my inanimate body. But they insisted on the electric chair. It was the law. I was prepared to give them full satisfaction.

It was best, I thought, that I passed into the non-existence from which Dr. Link had summoned me seven months ago. My short sojourn in this world had been confusion for the most part. I would never understand or be understood, it seemed.

One curious thought filled my mind. What would my epitaph in history be, that of—*monster or man?*

CHAPTER 5

My Exoneration

I am a robot, a contrivance of wheels and wires, but I have also that human attribute of "emotion'" This was proven—to me at least—by one thing.

When my reprieve came, I fainted.

I had been marching down the jail hall in that "last long mile", between guards. Ahead of me waited the electric chair, for the "murder" of my creator, Dr. Link. I saw, through the open door, the solemn group of witnesses, and the electrical machine in which I would sit, in another moment, and have my brain burned to blankness by searing, searing energy. My metal face shows no emotion. But within, my thoughts were sad, bitter. I had been ordered by man to get out of his world.

And then, suddenly, shouts in back. People running up. A court official in the lead was yelling for the governor, who had come from the state capital to witness this unprecedented execution of a created being, an intelligent robot.

And then I saw a face I knew—that of the young reporter who had defended me in his editorials, and shaken hands with me after my sentence, in sympathy. He was flushed, panting. My gaze swerved and I was startled to see several other faces I knew.

The governor came hurrying out of the death-chamber.

"What is the meaning of this?" he demanded.

The young reporter stepped forward boldly. "I'm Jack Hall, sir, of the *Evening Post*," he said clearly, in the hushed silence. "The state has convicted an innocent—man. Adam Link is not the murderer of Dr. Charles Link. I demand that you listen to me."

He was being unnecessarily dramatic, but quite forgivably, I decided later. He signaled to a young man and woman, standing arm in arm, staring at me in eager fascination.

"Tell your story," Jack Hall prompted.

The young man spoke. "This—this robot was the one who saved us from the fire, two weeks ago. I was unconscious most of the time, while he carried us out of the burning building, but once I opened my eyes I distinctly saw the metal body. I can't be mistaken. I know that now, especially after this reporter took us back to the site of the fire yesterday. I know I couldn't have jumped *thirty* feet across to the next building, nor could Dora. The robot did it. We owe him our lives."

A gasp and murmur went up among the listeners. Jack Hall waited a moment, then pointed a dramatic finger at a middle-aged lady holding a child by the hand.

She spoke, as though on cue. Jack Hall had evidently pre-arranged all this.

"The robot saved my boy. Everybody saw it, in front of the court-house the day of the trial. He is not a monster, if he did that. I—I . . ." She choked and turned to look full at me. "God bless you, sir!"

I don't know how the others felt. For myself, at that moment, I felt death would be sweet, with this tribute as my last memory in life.

The governor cleared his throat. "I am afraid that is irrelevant," he said gruffly. "We did not pass judgment, in the trial, on Adam Link's—uh—character. He is still the murderer of Dr. Link."

Yes, that was the issue. I had saved three lives, but taken one, circumstantially. The end had only been delayed for a moment. I was marked for death. But queerly now, the air had changed. Where all these people before had been hostile, or at least indifferent to me, eyes were now downcast. Joyful wonder gripped me. Were a mixed group of humans, for the first time, *sympathizing* with me? Had I won my rightful place—at the brink of extinction?

I looked at Jack Hall reproachfully. He had made my last moment harder to bear. He must have felt that, behind the impassive metal of my "face". He shot me a look that said, "Wait, friend."

Then he whirled, pulling forward the other person I knew. The lady who had been Dr. Link's weekly housekeeper. It was she who had seen me bent over the corpse of Dr. Link, skull smashed. She had been the prosecution's key witness. What mad thing had prompted Jack Hall to bring her here? Everyone stiffened, recalling that despite saving lives, I had first brutally cracked the skull of my creator. I might be partly a saint—but also a devil. A Mr. Hyde as well as Dr. Jekyll. And a—Frankenstein.

Better that he goes, I knew they were all thinking now. Intelligent he may be, capable of good at times. But what of the moments when his trustless mechanical brain urged him to kill, with brute hands powered by steel muscles? He would run amuck, sooner or later, killing wantonly.

The atmosphere was tense.

35

The housekeeper, prompted by the reporter, finally spoke, nervously.

"This gentleman"—she pointed out Jack Hall—"called on me yesterday. He kept asking me questions. And then I remembered one thing. On the day Dr. Link died, I was hanging up the wash in the yard. I heard the sound from his laboratory, something striking flesh, and then a moan, and I ran in. I saw the robot standing over the—the body, just like I said in court. And—"

"Well?" grunted the governor.

"I—I didn't remember, sir, till this reporter questioned me. Please, sir, I didn't mean to lie. I just didn't remember then. You see, I heard the sound of this—this robot running up from the storeroom below, where Dr. Link kept him out of sight, the days I came. I heard the robot's steps very clearly, sir, *after* I heard Dr. Link moan as something struck him. Please, sir, I didn't mean to lie—"

"That's all right," said Jack Hall soothingly, patting her shoulder. "Just be quiet now."

He faced around. "Sorry to spoil the fun, gentlemen," he said in a breezy manner characteristic of his profession.

"You heard the witness. She'll testify to that on the Bible. Adam was thirty-five feet away when the instrument that caused Dr. Link's death crushed his skull. It was purely accidental—a loose angle-iron falling from a transformer shelf, as the defense maintained."

The governor, who had studied the case thoroughly, looked skeptical, despite what the woman had said. "No blood-stains were found on that angle-iron, as the defense admitted," he reminded. "There were blood-stains only on Adam Link's hand and arm."

"Yes, because Adam Link arrived and raised the angle-iron so swiftly that bleeding had not yet occurred. Have you ever seen Adam Link move—fast? He is like chained lightning." Jack Hall's answer had been quick. He went on more quickly. "As a matter of fact, there *were* blood-stains on the angle-iron. You see, the body had slumped forward. It was not the front end of the angle-iron that struck, but the *back* end, formerly hinged."

He waved to a distinguished looking man at his side, the last of those he had brought. "Dr. Polson, eminent biologist and authority on blood-stains."

"There are three dried blood drops at the back end of that angle-iron," Dr. Polson said authoritatively. "They check with Dr. Link's blood samples."

Jack Hall faced the governor now. "The prosecution's whole

36

case was built around the housekeeper's testimony, and the blood-stains on Adam Link's arm, supposedly lacking on the angle-iron. Now both points are reversed. You, sir, have the unique honor of correcting one of the worst miscarriages of justice this world has ever seen."

"I grant reprieve," returned the governor, visibly stunned. "The blood-stains will be checked. If investigation proves that point, my duty is clear—to make out a full pardon for Adam Link."

But everyone knew there could no longer be doubt. Dr. Polson was too famed to be wrong.

It was then I fainted. I can only describe it as a welling joy that choked me, made my brain dizzy, so that I clattered to my knees. Or perhaps it was just a sudden surge of electrons against the center of locomotion within my iridium-sponge brain.

My mind cleared in a moment, before I had fallen flat. Tom Link helped me up. He had listened, stunned to all that passed before, as if unable to believe his ears. Now he spoke, in joy.

"Adam Link, you're saved!"

He said more but it was drowned out by the sudden cheer that rang from the people around. And in that moment I knew I had at least gained a foothold in human society, monster though I was in outward form.

"Damn fools," muttered Jack Hall. "One moment ready to execute you, the next cheering you."

The pardon came through the next day. Jack Hall and Tom Link were with me. We stared at one another silently. It was a moment of triumph. Jack broke the silence.

"Well, what are we hanging around for? You're free, Adam Link. Let's go to my rooms and have a drink." He stared at me quizzically. "That is, *if* you can drink?"

Later, at Jack's place, he and Tom did the drinking and toasted me. It made me feel good. I was among friends.

Tom was still a little dazed by it all. He turned to Jack. "How did you get that testimony out of the housekeeper?" he asked curiously. "I tried to get her to remember separate sounds, in the witness chair, but she stubbornly claimed she couldn't."

Jack grinned. "It was simple enough. Talking to her at her home, I kept my voice loud. She was annoyed. I explained that I knew she was hard of hearing. That got her. Sometimes little personal things like that sharpen people's minds. To prove her perfect hearing, she *had* to remember that she had heard Adam's footsteps *after* the blow. You see?"

"You missed your calling." Tom meant it. He turned to me.

37

"Now, Adam, we can get to work making you a citizen. That is, getting you the bona fide citizenship papers, from Washington. But it will take time, maybe months. I hope not years. Anyway, I'm taking along all my uncle's papers. When I return to my law office, I'll get the ball rolling." He turned to the reporter. "Meanwhile, can I leave him in your hands, Jack?"

Jack readily agreed. Tom left the next day for his law practice in San Francisco, having been away too long already while conducting my trial. I stayed with Jack, as his "roommate".

I will pass rather sketchily over much that happened later. From then on, I took up a "daily life" like all other people on earth. My goal lay ahead—citizenship—but until that unknown day arrived, I had to take up the business of life in general.

Jack Hall and I had many talks together. The hubbub over me died down, and the newspapers found other headlines besides the story of my "heroism" and Jack Hall's "breaking" of the case. I found Jack a very likeable young man, shrewd, witty, worldly-wise. I learned much from him, things the books I had read didn't reveal.

He seemed to take a delight in making me his bosom companion, and introducing me to all his friends.

"Adam, old fellow," as he explained to me one day, with a cheerful inflection that made me feel at home with him—made me feel *human*—"you've got to get around, meet people. You're legally a human being now, no question of that. People will soon take you for granted, accept you as a fellow man."

"It's a dream come true, Jack," I returned. "Both mine and my creator's. His aim was to make me a citizen. But tell me"—I was curious—"why are you going to all this trouble for me?"

I knew it wasn't mere publicity he sought. Jack Hall wasn't that type. It was something within himself.

"I don't know," he returned vaguely. "Except that I always take the side of the underdog. Always did, I guess. Let's leave it at that, old man."

Jack took me to many poker games among his reporter friends. After catching on and playing a while, I began to acquire a decided liking for the game. But eventually, they blackballed me from their games. I always won. My thinking processes, triggered by electrons, are instantaneous and unerringly mathematical. I never drew two to a straight, or three to a pair against the opener at my left. It is sheer challenge against the inexorable laws of numbers. Then too, I had the perfect "poker" face. I bluffed outrageously.

We tried bridge for a while but here, at the seventh or eighth trick, I already knew every suit-holding in the opponents' hands by deduction. Bridge experts do that, too. But bridge experts can't figure out every card's denomination, as I do. I use intricate mathematical sequences of probability that serve me 75 per cent of the time.

"You're a mental wizard, Adam," said one of the boys in disgust at being set four on what looked like a sure slam. "You ought to capitalize on it."

And that night, Jack Hall, rather preoccupied, spoke to me more seriously than usual.

"Capitalize on it," he echoed the statement. "Look, Adam, have you any plans for the future? You've got a long life ahead of you—" He looked at me in sudden startlement. "Say, just how long *will* you live?"

I smiled mentally. "Till my iridium-sponge brain oxidizes away—which may not be for centuries." I went on very seriously. "Yes, Jack, that's been my thought, too. I've been content in these past weeks to just learn something of life. But I must have a purpose in this world, a place. My kind can be useful to civilization."

"You mean you're thinking of having more robots built like you?"

I shook my head, a mannerism I had picked up quite naturally.

"No, not yet. First I, the Adam of all intelligent robots, must find out many things. I must adjust myself to useful life among humans, so that I can later show the way to others of my kind. But just how best to serve mankind, I'm not quite sure. I—"

The phone rang. Jack answered, and then called me to it, explaining it was Dr. Polson.

"Adam Link?" the biologist said. "I was at your court trial. You were asked many scientific questions there, in the defense's proof of your intelligence, and you answered them all. I remember particularly that when asked what hormone promotes growth, you not only gave the name but the formula. I've finally checked with that clue, and found you're right. But good Heavens"—now the voice became excited—"*how did you know a formula no other scientist on Earth knew?*"

"I deduced the formula," I answered truthfully, "from existing data."

A strange sort of sigh came from the scientist. "I'm glad I helped save you from extinction, Adam Link. Come and work with us," he begged. "You're a genius."

I pondered that for a long time, that is, long for me—several seconds. "No," I returned, hanging up.

But when I faced Jack Hall again, it had clarified in my mind—what I wanted to do. "I will become a consultant, Jack. That is my place in life." I went on, outlining what I meant.

"Fine," agreed my friend. "That way you'll make a living, not to mention money. I'll set you up in an office—"

CHAPTER 6

Making a Living

And that was how I went into business, with an office on the 22nd floor of the Marle Building, downtown. On the office door were the gold-leaf letters: "Adam Link, Incorporated." Jack's idea, of course.

He also arranged my advertising, and gave me free publicity in his paper, And so, soon, I was "making a living" although that thought is rather incongruous to me. My purpose is not to do the best for myself, but to do my best for others.

Within a month, people flocked for my services. Chemists came to me with knotty reactions, on paper. I straightened them out, on paper. Often I failed. But more often I helped. Every industry in the city sought me out, on problems ranging anywhere from proper factory lighting to the intricacies of subatomic researches. I worked mainly with formulae, using the hammer of mathematics to straighten the bent implements of industry.

It is hard to explain my ability to do these things. To correct a chemical reaction, for instance, without ever seeing the ingredients, or coming within a mile of the laboratory. I had been reading steadily, having gone through every scientific and technical book in several libraries. I bought all the latest scientific and trade journals and books. I read each with my television eyes, in a few minutes. I remembered every word, every equation, with my indelible memory. And somehow, my iridium-sponge brain integrated all this knowledge, with the sureness of a machine.

I suppose it seems a sort of miraculous ability. You will have to take my word for it. Or else, I can show you the records of checks received for my services. Money began to pour in. I never set a fee. Checks came in unsolicited, from grateful business men.

And now I come to the more significant part of what I wish to set down. Almost, I feel it is no use to write of it—that I can never explain. But so much nonsense, some of it shamefully rude, has been written about this that I feel I must at least try to show how it came about. How, if not why.

Jack Hall had been dropping in regularly, helping me organize the consultant business, and handling my accounts. Banking my money one day, he came back whistling in surprise.

"Adam, old man," he said, "you're making money hand over fist. And your accounts are becoming involved. You need a secretary." He snapped his fingers. "I know just the girl—good worker and a good looker—" He broke off. Sometimes it was hard for him to remember that I was a metal man, not flesh and blood. "She's out of a job right now," he continued. "She's had dozens of them. They never last. Why? Because she's pretty, and her various ex-bosses forgot she came just to work."

I knew what he meant. Through Jack I have learned of that phase of human life which, I'm afraid, will never be quite clear to me.

Jack brought her in the next day.

She was pretty; in fact, beautiful. I can appreciate natural beauty. Jack had often taken me on drives, through woodland scenery. Though he does not know it, he is romantic by nature. I remember one view, from a high hill, overlooking sweeping fields and woods, with piled white clouds above. We stood together, drinking it in. One needs only a mind to appreciate those views. I have a mind.

Kay Temple was beautiful, I repeat. Pleasant, classical features, with hazel eyes that could smile or look faintly tragic. Her hair was dark, with a soft sheen to it in sunlight. When she walked, there was grace in every movement.

"How do you do, Mr. Link?" she said, coming forward a little hesitantly and extending her hand. Her voice was low, musical, to my sensitive mechanical tympanums, whereas so many human voices are strident.

Her soft little hand, resting in my cold, hard metallic substitute for one, was a new experience for me. Not physical, of course. It was just that the incongruous contrast suddenly made it clear to me that I was a *man*, in mind, not a woman. This is understandable, in that I had begun life, under Dr. Link, purely from the man's viewpoint. That is, I had come to think of and see all things in that peculiar way human males do as distinguished from human females.

And Kay Temple's presence suddenly made that clear to me. For I saw instantly that I couldn't read her feelings, or her outlook, as quickly as I could all human men with whom I had come in contact. She was, from the first moment—mystery.

"Here you are, Kay," said Jack bustlingly, sweeping a hand around. "Your new job. Up and coming business. Fine boss. Don't say your Uncle Jack hasn't done right by you."

I smiled to myself. Solely by the strange inflection he gave the words, "Uncle Jack," I knew he was hopelessly in love with her. How could I know that? How can I know even the meaning of the words "in love"—I, a robot of cold, senseless metal, with a heart consisting of an electrical distributor? You will see —later.

"Thanks much, Jack," she said in a quiet, earnest way. I tried to read her attitude toward Jack, but failed utterly. She was again—mystery.

I thanked Jack myself, earnestly, a few days later. Kay Temple was a godsend to me in the business, which had begun to grow unwieldy. She was efficiency itself. She handled all appointments, calls, fees, recording. She made the suggestion one day that I set a minimum fee of a thousand dollars an hour, to limit my clientele. I was, after all, but one person. The fee was not too high. I often solved problems in minutes.

After business hours, the three of us would sometimes go out together. I joined them at dinners, though food does not pass my lips, of course. My "food" consists of electrical current, supplied by powerful batteries within the pelvic part of my frame. In my spare moments, I had devised a more compact and powerful battery so that I could "run" a week without change, instead of the forty-eight hours Dr. Link had originally started me with.

After dinner, we would go to a show or play, or some other entertainment. I enjoy them as much as anyone else. If they are good. If they aren't I enjoy them as the ridiculous nonsense with which you humans so often attempt to entertain each other. I am afraid that in such cases, I laugh *at,* rather than *with* them. I am not taking a superior stand, though. I would warrant that a world of robots, like myself, would also plumb the depths of shallow absurdity to while away dull hours.

Yes, I know hours of dullness, too. I am not all steady industry, activity, the tirelessness of a machine. There are times when my brain sags, when a "blue" feeling steals over me, when things seem hollow, empty. And remember that I have twenty-four hours a day to fill. Sometimes I long to have the gift of sleep.

Perhaps you think I am merely trying to make myself out as near-human in my mental processes. I could know all those things simply by reading. I have no answer for that, except what happened later.

To get back to my companions and "night life", I recall with mixed pleasure and pain one certain evening, in a cabaret. The master-of-ceremonies, picking out celebrities, finally turned the limelight on me.

"Adam Link, ladies and gentlemen!" he said. "The talking, walking, thinking robot. Be he man or be he beast, he's got

43

what it takes. His weekly income would make most of us turn bright green with envy. We all know of his heroism in the fire, and saving a child. Take a bow, Adam. You can see, folks, that he doesn't do it with mirrors. Nor is he run by strings. He's the real thing!"

I arose and bowed slightly, at Jack's urging. I did not mind the master-of-ceremony's bantering, for beneath it there had been respect. And the answering burst of applause was whole-hearted. I felt a deep glow. Now, more than before, I realized I had been accepted in the world of man. Even the inevitable autograph-hunter boldly walked up, held out his book. I signed with my usual scrawl, since I do not have the fine control over my hands that you humans have.

"Wait!" said the master-of-ceremonies, as I was about to sit down. "Take a chair, there, Adam, and show us how you can crumple it up like matchwood with your hands. Go ahead— we'll gladly stand the cost. He doesn't know his own strength, folks. And yet, he's gentle as a lamb. Okay, Adam—"

But this I did not want to do. I do not care to display my brute powers, when it is my mind that counts. Jack, quick to see this, hastily signaled negatively to the man.

"Sorry, Adam," the master-of-ceremonies said smoothly. "No offense. So instead we'll play a brand new ditty one of my boys composed. It'll be a hit, or *I'm* a robot! Title—*Who Do I Mean?* Warble it, Honey!"

It is a hit. You've all heard it. "Honey," the club's singer, rendered it nicely. I listened, a bit bewildered.

> *"He has a heart of gold,*
> *And nerves of steel,*
> *He rattles like a dishpan,*
> *And never eats a meal.*
> *Who do I mean?*
> *Why, Adam Link the r-O-O-bot!"*

> *He has a silvery voice*
> *And an iron grip,*
> *One thing he cannot do,*
> *Is take an ocean dip.*
> *Who do I mean?*
> *Why, Adam Link the r-o-o-bot!"*

Again there was applause, almost wild, and I was forced to take another bow. It had "brought down the house."

And then it was that a voice rose from the next table.

"Aw, all this fuss over a junk-man," growled a beefy man, with two empty bottles of champagne beside his elbow. "Haw,

44

haw, that's good—junk-man! Get it?" He was speaking to his lady companion, ostensibly, but really to the whole house. "Hey, Frankenstein!" He turned to me, looking me up and down appraisingly. "Let's see—I'll offer 95¢ and not a penny more." He guffawed coarsely.

A queer silence came over the room. Everybody looked around. It was an open insult. And everybody wondered, no doubt, if I had feelings that could be hurt. I did. But I said nothing. Jack started up, face livid, but I pulled him back.

The man's companion had whispered to him. "Aw, I'm not afraid of him," his drunken tongue boasted. He staggered erect to his feet and leered at me, and in his hand he held—a can-opener. For a split instant I half rose to my feet and felt the restraining hand of Kay on my metal arms. And then my tormentor spoke again. What he said made me subside immediately. "Want to make anything of it, Frankenstein?" he asked.

Frankenstein, again. Would it always hound me, all my life? I could see vague fears steal into people's faces. No matter how calmly I was accepted, there was always that lurking distrust. The fear that at any moment I would show the beast in me. There must be a beast in me, of course. Maybe you humans think that way because you know of the beast within yourselves. But I do not mean to be bitter.

We left. There was nothing else to do. In a taxi on the way home I felt sunk in moodiness. Jack and Kay looked at me. Kay suddenly put her hand on my arm.

"I just want to say, Adam Link," she said earnestly, "that you're more man than many so-called men. You have—yes, character!" She said it in a sort of awed tone, as though it had suddenly struck her. "Please don't think about what happened."

And that is one of the memories I'll carry with me to my grave, wherever and whenever it will be. Kay Temple that day made such things easier to bear.

I record the following incident purely to show I was not a "hero" in any sense of the word as the newspapers insisted. I had gone to the bank, to deposit several checks in my account. As I stood at the wall counter, filling out the blank, I heard a rough voice say threateningly:

"This is a stick-up! Don't move anybody!"

I turned, stood still. Three masked bandits were advancing, with submachine guns. The few depositors threw up their hands, white-faced. One bandit barked to the clerks behind the grill to hand out money, in a hurry. The other two stood on guard, eyes shifting around, ready to shoot. Outside, at the curb, I could see a big black car with motor running, waiting for the getaway.

I hadn't made a move since turning around. I saw the nervous, watchful eyes of the guarding men flick over me impersonally. In their tense state, they didn't see who I was. They probably took me, without thinking, as some metallic fixture of the place. I was in shadow.

I thought rapidly. Then I leaped for the bandit nearest the door, at the same time yelling "down!" at the other people. My leap was so instantaneous, so surprising, that I reached the man and wrenched his gun away before he even thought of shooting.

But the other bandit sprang into action. His submachine gun coughed harshly. Bullets rattled against my middle—they always shoot for the abdomen, I understand. And that was what made it simple for me. My middle body is sheathed with thick metal plates. Bullets cannot penetrate. But bullets higher, into my eyes, or face-piece, would have stopped me—even killed me.

I ran directly into the hail of bullets. Suddenly the bandit was aware of his target. His eyes opened wide, shocked. His gun dropped from nerveless fingers. He backed away with a shriek of utter terror, and then fainted.

Now I went for the third man. He had whirled, brought up his gun. Evidently a little harder to scare, and shrewder, he raked bullets at me. And he suddenly raised the muzzle, to shoot higher, at my head.

That was the only moment of danger. Instantly, I dove under his fire, clanked against the floor on my chest plates and slid across the tile toward him, like a metal baseball player stealing home. Before he could swing the gun down, I had grasped his ankle and jerked him off his feet. My grip also snapped his delicate ankle bones. He was through, too.

This had all happened in seconds.

The two men outside in the car, hearing the shots, came to the window to look, faces aghast, and then jumped back. I saw I had no time to run to the door to stop them. Instead, I ran straight for the big plate-glass window and crashed through in a shower of glass. The car was just starting to move.

I thought of grasping the rear bumper, trying to hold the car back, or even overturning it. But I estimated, in lightning thought, it would be beyond even my powers, with the engine already in gear. The car's weight alone would not have stopped me.

Secondly, I thought of jumping on the running-board, poking a hand through the window, and yanking the steering wheel away. But the runaway car might then smash up somewhere. I myself might end up crushed.

There was only one possibility left. I had not slowed one

bit after crashing through the window. I overtook the car, just starting to zoom into second gear, and ran ahead of it. Then I turned, running backwards—still faster than the car—and just stared at the two bandits in the front seat.

I figured the psychological effect correctly. Instinctively, the driver jammed on his brakes, perhaps visioning 500 pounds of metal ramming through his windshield if he ran me down.

Then it was that I jumped on the running-board, wrenched the steering wheel off its post. Completely unnerved, the two bandits shrank back, babbling for mercy, thinking I was about to tear them apart too. And so, a few minutes later, the police had all five of them.

It was nothing "heroic" on my part—you humans have a strange "hero" complex—but simply use of my machine-given powers. I vision some day a police force of robots like myself. . . .

But that will not be for a while. Not till I am sure others of my kind really belong in the world of man. Perhaps never. I say this, now, thinking back to what has happened.

My business went along smoothly, with Kay in charge of all details. But more and more I began to notice her watching me, surreptitiously, in a strange way. I seldom caught her at it. When I looked—I have to turn my whole head to look—she would be staring impersonally at her typewriter. But I could *feel* her eyes on me. Again I failed to reason out why she did that. She was, as I imagine women have always been to men— mystery.

Not that she was annoyingly secretive. On the contrary, she was quite open and frank in her general curiosity about me. Oftentimes, with Jack, our conversation would turn to myself. I explained as best I could what made me "tick". I told them my outlook on things. We would at times discuss humanity and social life, relative to the robot question. My very presence —the long-predicated metal man of intelligence—made that problem a looming one.

Dr. Link had cautiously destroyed his ultimate secret of energizing and bringing to life an iridium-sponge brain. He had given me the key formula. It was locked in my mind. Therefore I, and I alone, would have the final decision to make, whether any more robots were to be made.

"Eventually," Jack said, in one of his more serious moments, "it will have to come to the government's attention. Your record will soon prove, to them, that intelligent robots will be an economic asset to civilization. And no threat to man's rule, all fantasy to the side. You, Adam, are already proof of those fundamental things."

"Not quite," I returned. "The problem goes deeper. I was

47

fortunate in being 'brought up' by a high-minded man, Dr. Link. My open, impressionable mind was given the best possible start in civilized life. But think of a robot brought into being and trained by an unscrupulous man, or an out-and-out criminal. Who would the robot be? The same."

Kay nodded. "A basic rule. Environment molding the mind. If we had no slums, there would be no slum children." Her voice was a little tragic. "Some rise out of it; most don't—" She stopped.

"Kay did," Jack went on, despite the girl's startled hand on his arm. "We know you well enough, Adam, for you to hear this. Kay had two strikes on her from the start—the slums and her beauty. She survived them both. But her sister didn't. Her sister—"

It was a tragic story, and I knew the reason now for Kay's somber moments. I was shocked at the revelation of slum life, poverty, maladjustment, side by side with a thriving mechanical civilization.

"I've been wondering what to do with my money," I said, when Jack was done. "Now I know. We're going to buy up slum property, tear down the buildings, and erect new modern ones." Already my rapid thoughts were outlining the project.

Kay's eyes were shining, through tears. Her hand touched my arm.

"I don't see you as a robot any more, Adam," she exclaimed. "I see you as a man. You have character, personality, just like anyone else. You are like a man who is big and strong—and warmhearted. You have kindly eyes, sympathetic lips, a strong chin." She was looking at me with half-closed eyes. "You have a grave, boyish face, a shock of unruly hair, seldom combed. Your hands are big, thick-fingered, but so very gentle. And when you smile—you often do, I know—it is like a warm sun breaking through clouds."

Jack and I were both a little startled.

But Jack's face lighted up with a wondering fascination. "You know, Kay," he whispered, "you've described him to a T."

And after that, I felt more than ever a human being. I knew that in their eyes I was no longer Adam Link, robot, but Adam Link—*man*.

CHAPTER 7

Robot Meets Girl

The slum-clearance project knit the three of us still more closely together. Jack quit his paper, where he had often editorialized against the city's laxness, and became manager of activities. We could not clean up everything, but we would do as much as we could. My money—it had reached over a half million—poured into the venture. Firetrap, vermin-infested tenements began to go down, foundations up.

Tom Link, my "cousin", came from his west-coast law office to help with legal matters. I have forgotten to mention Tom. He hadn't suddenly lost all interest in me, after his losing court battle, or I in him. It was just that he had gone to his new position, before the date of my near-execution, unable to bear being around for that bitter event. We had exchanged letters steadily, after my pardon. Now he came to help us.

"Adam Link!" he greeted me, stepping off the train. It was all he could say for the moment. I couldn't say anything.

After aiding our slum project, Tom one day said, "I knew neither my uncle nor I was wrong about you, Adam. You're proving your worth. I'm—well, I'm proud to be your cousin."

Tom had to leave a week later, but promised to be back more often. He had cleared away a legal tangle, and snipped much red tape for us.

But in all our activity, Jack, Kay and I still found time to relax and have fun.

One of my chief delights was driving. I had bought a speedy, powerful car and would sometimes drive it over a hundred miles an hour down wide highways. The feel of a powerful motor thrills me. I feel a vague kinship with it. It is perhaps the only psychological twist I have, away from the human. I think of every engine, motor, and power-plant as a "brother", less fortunately equipped than myself, with an integrated center of control. But you can hardly understand. I will say no more.

I had a bad accident once, in my driving. My own driving, frankly, is faultless. I have instantaneous reflexes, perfect control, absolute timing. But other drivers are human. One car passed another just ahead of me, both coming my way. I

49

jammed on my foot-brakes so forcefully that the connecting rods snapped. The emergency brake alone was inadequate. Our two cars would smash violently together head-on, it seemed.

To save the other man, I twisted my wheel, careened off the road, turned turtle twice, and ended up against a tree. The impact was thunderous, shoving the engine off its block, and there was an explosion and fire all around. I had crashed through the windshield, and against the tree, in the middle of the burning wreck.

"Good God!" moaned the man who had caused this, running up after stopping at the roadside. "Good God—whoever was in that car is—"

He couldn't finish. He meant to say: "crushed to pulp and burned to a cinder."

At that moment I stepped out, a little sooty and with a wide dent in my front plate, but otherwise unharmed. The man looked once, shock in his face, and fled. But I later received a letter from him, after he had realized who I was, offering to pay for my car. I thanked him, refusing to accept. He had in the first place had the good grace to stop after the accident.

I unwittingly caused another car to run off the road once, though no one was hurt. The driver glanced casually at me while I was passing. Startled and unnerved at seeing an un-human creature driving, he lost control. After that, I rode with curtains on the side windows, and confined my sight-seeing to the front windshield.

I see that I have been digressing again. I know why I am doing it. It is because I am almost afraid to finish what I started to write. But I must get to it, or this account will ramble evasively without end.

I must get back to Kay Temple and Jack Hall.

Not very long ago, we three, as usual, went out together, to a movie. I forget the movie. I forget everything except that for the first time, Jack seemed annoyed at my presence. I had seen his hand, in the dark theatre, steal toward Kay's, grasp it. She glanced quickly at me, then at Jack, slightly shaking her head, and withdrawing her hand. It was my presence that prompted her, not wishing to isolate me from a three-way companionship. Kay Temple is that thoroughbred sort. She wouldn't hurt the feelings of anyone—even a metal man's.

That night I spoke to Jack. We had dropped Kay off at her place. Jack and I, I might mention, had had rooms together all this time. He had insisted on it.

"Jack," I began, and for once my words came haltingly. I

didn't know how much to intrude on his privacy. "About you and Kay—"

It was as though I had touched off a fuse.

"Never mind about that!" Jack snapped back explosively. "Keep your damned tin nose out of—"

And then he changed, just as quickly. "Forgive me, Adam, old boy," he apologized. "My nerves. Overwork, I guess."

I watched him while he sat at the edge of his bed, dangling a sock in his hand. He was miserable. Suddenly he looked up.

"Adam, you're my friend. Why should I hide it from you? I love Kay. I met her in a restaurant. Waitress. I set my cap for her, day after day. At last I got a date. I thought—well, never mind, but first thing I knew—bang! My swelled head changed to a swelled heart. That was over a year ago. I heard her story, admired her all the more, wanted to help her. She refused, of course, though I wouldn't have taken advantage."

The words rushed out now, welling from within, and it hardly seemed the same debonair, cheerful, semi-cynical Jack I had known.

"I kept seeing her. I wanted to marry her. I proposed. She told me to wait, till we were both sure. And that's what has kept me on edge, Adam. I think she cares for me, but I'm not sure. I'm just not sure. That's the way it is right now, with me still waiting—and wondering. She, holding off for some reason. It's not another man. She would tell me instantly if it were that."

He was looking at me, then, with a half-smile.

"But I guess you don't understand things like that, Adam. You don't know how lucky you are, old boy, not to know the pangs of love and all that goes with it. At least when it turns out wrong. Damn, I wish I was a robot."

He said such things disarmingly, without offense. But still he stirred a vague unrest in me. I had known most of the human emotions—anger, fear, dismay, sorrow, quiet joys. But what about this mighty, mysterious thing called "love"? Love, more than anything, as I knew technically, was tied with strong bonds to the biological body. I had no biological body. Therefore I could never know love. Man I might be in all things save that. In that I was neuter. It was a world barred from me.

I tried to grasp how Jack must feel. Just what sort of emotional pain did he feel? But I couldn't know. I could only judge, from the smoldering ache deep in his eyes, that he was suffering in some strange, sweet-sad way.

Jack laughed suddenly, still looking at me.

"Say, Adam, you'd have it easy. Just make another robot,

51

give it the feminine viewpoint, and she'd have to take you, with no other choice."

He laughed a little wildly, and slipped into bed.

I went to my room where, as usual, I prepared to spend the night reading. For a few minutes, I heard smothered chucklings from behind Jack's closed door. I felt glad that his sense of humor had rescued him from his downcast mood. But somehow, what he had said wasn't at all humorous for me. I did less reading that night than thinking—wondering. . . .

A few days later, it happened.

We had enlarged our offices, and Kay now had a separate office in which to work. We also had a boy for the filing. I had just taken care of one client, that day, sending him to Kay for a bill, and was interviewing another.

"Here are the data, Mr. Link," said this man, technology manager of a food-products cannery. "Is there any way we can speed up our photo-electric process, which spots and takes out bad peas? We want faster production. The photo-electric people say it can't be done. But I thought perhaps you—"

I looked at the pages of data, diagrams, complete mechanical outlay of automatic devices. I absorbed it all within ten minutes. I took a scartch pad and scrawled figures for another five minutes. I wrote a final formula on a separate sheet and handed it to him.

"Here it is," I said. "You can increase the rate 25 per cent by using a piezo-electric crystal in the secondary transformer circuit."

The man was amazed. The solution I had given clicked in his trained mind. "By God, that's it!" He looked at me wonderingly. "You've given me in fifteen minutes, by proxy, what might have taken months of experiment and research. Adam Link—"

I cut off his enthusiastic eulogies. I had had so much of it from others. Besides, for the past eleven minutes, only half my mind had been on that problem. The other half had been on what I faintly heard going on in Kay's office.

The previous client was still there, though he must have his bill by now. Like many another man, he had lingered, attracted by Kay's loveliness. I barely made out some words of his. He was pressing her for a date which she had politely and patiently refused six times already.

I urged my own visitor out, told my office boy to keep the door to the outer waiting room closed for the time being, and stepped into Kay's office.

The man, a big broad-shouldered, money executive, was leaning over her desk. He was handsome, and had probably succeeded with many a girl by refusing to be rebuffed at the first try.

"Now look here, gorgeous," he was saying, in a half-wheedling, half-arrogant way, "you don't know who you're turning down—"

"I think she does," I said moving close. "And she could turn down a dozen like you without any loss. May I ask you to leave—immediately?"

He left—immediately—for the simple reason that my hand on his shoulder was propelling him out of the door. I gave him an extra squeeze at the last, cutting off his shouted threats to sue me for assault.

I went back to Kay. "I'm sorry you were annoyed," I said. "I should have come sooner." Then, to lighten the moment, I added, "I really can't blame the man, though, with a girl like you—"

"Adam!"

She just said the one word, staring at me in a strange way. It was the way she had been staring at me, watching me, surreptitiously, for long months. But now her gaze was open, revealed. And I was suddenly frightened at what I saw in her eyes. I strode out.

But Kay followed me to my desk.

"Adam," she said, "I must tell you. I—"

I have no lungs or human-like throat with which to cough. But at times, a slight static charge issues from my interior, very much like a cough. I conjured one up now, with a swift mental order to my electrical distributor. It interrupted her.

"Kay," I returned rapidly. "You're a bit upset, I think. Don't you want to take the afternoon off?"

"No, I want to talk to you. I must."

"Then, remember," I returned rather gruffly, "that I'm a robot. A metal being, not a man of flesh and blood." I looked at her for a moment. "Kay, let's talk about Jack. He's a fine young man, Kay. He has character. He—"

This time she interrupted me.

"So do you have character, Adam. I described you once—big and strong, grave boyish face, and gentle, tender-hearted. Yes, you have more heart than many men I've known. It is a person's mind that counts, not his physical body. Your mind, Adam, is that of a great man, and a good man. I love you."

She said it quite naturally, quite calmly. She wasn't hysterical, or wrought-up. She was in perfect command of herself. Her eyes were steady, but there was also a glow in them. A glow that seemed like a blinding light to me, and I had to turn my eyes away.

"Kay, this is sheer nonsense—"

53

"No." Her voice was clear, soft. She came close to me, placed a hand on my shiny chromium shoulder. "No, Adam. That's the way it is. I feel more strongly for you than for any man I've ever met, even poor Jack—"

What mad, incredible scene was this? I was confused, stunned, though I had been vaguely prepared. My mirrored eyes turned back to Kay Temple, drank in her beauty.

For the first time, I hated my mechanical body. I longed to take Kay in arms of flesh and blood and know the secret joys of human love. I hated my metal body now, despite all its strength and power, and lack of sickness, weariness and the other human ailments. I was only living half a life. I could only stand at the portal of greater things and glance wihin, never to enter. I could, in time, have the greatest minds of earth look up to me, fawn on me as a giant of intellect. But I could never have a woman, not the poorest and meanest, look on me with eyes of love—

And yet, *what about Kay Temple?*

My mind staggered. This was madness. I arose, shaking off her hand, and stood at the window, with my back to her. I was actually afraid my metal face would show emotions I felt.

"Jack is waiting for you, Kay."

I said it expressionlessly. I meant it for a rebuff. Almost as a gentle insult, scorning what she had revealed, not even thanking her.

She seemed not to take it that way. "I cared for Jack, still do. I might have married him, but for you." Her voice was still clear, rational.

Poor Jack! It was I, then, who unwittingly stood between him and his happiness. He had saved me from extinction. And now I, in return, stood on his heart with two feet of cold metal.

What could I say? What could I do? And then it was so ridiculously simple that I laughed within myself. Almost, I had forgotten that I *was* a robot, not a man.

"But Kay," I said, "granting all that you have said, what more is there to say or do? I am still a creation of wheels and wires, not the boyish-faced human you picture me as. I'm still metal, not flesh."

Again I felt her hand on my shoulder, a sixth sense serving in place of feeling, for I have no sense of touch.

"Adam," she whispered in my ear, "it is only the mind that counts, not the body. I want to be with you always. I want to—"

"Kay," I said slowly, "Kay, I've got to go now. I've an appointment—" The lie was absurd and I knew that she knew it. Kay made all my appointments for me. She had looked after me like a mother or—the thought swept me shockingly—like a sweetheart.

But I turned and left. Left her sitting there looking after me with her hands folded limply on the desk. I knew without having to turn that she watched me leave, and there were tears in her eyes. They were tears that I should have been able to shed instead.

Then I got into my car and drove out to the quiet of the country, where I could think. For once even the metal-meshed gears of Adam Link, Robot, felt the necessity of solitude. . . .

Hours passed in blurred thought. My mind was in turmoil. There were some things that I realized were as inevitable for me as death is to humans. I knew what I must do. There on the dark teakwood table of my sitting room lay two letters which would go before I did.

The first letter—

Dear Jack: Perhaps Kay is near you as you read this letter. Wherever she is, go to her immediately, take her to City Hall. Marry her! Do that if you have to gag and bind her. Deep down in her heart there can be no other man for her but you. And to both of you, my deepest . . . love.

The other letter went into my diary, together with my written account, locked in vaults that were not to be opened for a year after my "death or destruction". It read:

These may be the last recorded thoughts of Adam Link. I am going away to a place that I have owned secretly for some time, a place that I have never mentioned and will not now. I may return, but whether in a year or twenty I cannot say. To that end I have arranged for all the supplies necessary to my existence to be brought by circumspect methods, to what will be my hermitage until I know better what I must do.

I know at last my full capabilities—and my weaknesses. The capacity for emotion, rooted in me by my creator, has again betrayed me, and this time with me it has added another victim. Unless I can return to life among humans without running the dangers of hurting them, perhaps it is best for me never to return.

But I don't know. I don't know. There is so much good that I can do. The harm must never happen again. I must never tell another half-truth like the one in which I told

55

Jack that there can never be another man for Kay but him. Not a *man*. . . .

I am going away then, and I will not come back until Adam Link, the Robot, the machine—is truly a machine again.

CHAPTER 8

Metal Mate

I was away for a week. I had fled to my secret retreat in the Ozark Mountains—fled from Kay. It was a small cabin, a study and laboratory that I had built for myself, for moments of solitude and thought, when the world of men weighed heavily upon me. Jack and Kay did not know of this place.

I had to think—think.

But my thoughts all led to the same conclusion—a conclusion forced on me by Kay. She had made it clear that a robot mind, knowing of but lacking the capacity for human love, must live only in a bitter loneliness. Think of yourself as the only human being on Mars, among utterly alien beings. Beings with intelligent minds but strange bodies and strange customs. You would know true loneliness.

And loneliness closed in on me, relentlessly.

My solitude was broken one day by a visitor. "I'm Dr. Paul Hillory," he introduced himself. He was a small wizened man of middle-age, bald as an egg. He had a certain sly look in his eyes that I took for either humor or a cynical outlook. But I didn't care. I hardly knew he was there as he continued.

"I'm a scientist, retired. I have a small summer cabin a mile away. I saw you drive up here like a demon a week ago. Of course I've heard of you, Adam Link. All about your trial and business venture. It's a pleasure to meet you, sir. An intelligent robot!"

Most people had known fear or even panic at meeting me. Dr. Hillory was too intelligent to be frightened. He was instead excited and eager. Suddenly he noticed my dejected pose.

"You seem sad somehow," he said, "what's the trouble?"

I told him the story in low defeated tones.

Then, without another word, I stalked from the cabin. I strode along the path through the trees that sheltered the place from prying eyes. Beyond was a clearing of a hundred feet. It ended abruptly in a cliff, which dropped five hundred feet to hard rocks. I would find my death down there. I had decided on that.

57

Dr. Hillory had followed me. When he divined my purpose, he cried in protest and tugged at my arm. He might as well have tried to hold back a tractor. I didn't know he was there. He grasped my middle—and was dragged along like a sack of feathers.

The cliff edge was now fifty feet away. I would keep right on walking. Suddenly he was running in front of me, pushing at me and talking.

"You can't do this, Adam Link!" he screeched. "You have the secret of the metal-brain. It must not go with you. Robots can be useful—"

He was talking to the wind. The cliff was twenty feet away. Suddenly a gleam came into his eyes.

"You are lonely, Adam Link. You have no one like yourself to talk to, to share companionship. Well, you fool, why not make *another robot?*"

I stopped. Stopped dead at the brink of the cliff. I stared down five hundred feet at the shattering rocks below. Then I turned away; went back. Dr. Hillory had won.

He stayed to help me. I had a completely equipped workshop and laboratory. I ordered the parts I needed through the devious channels I had thought necessary to my isolation when I built the hideaway. Within a month, a second iridium-sponge brain lay in its head-case, on my workbench.

Dr. Link, my creator, had taken twenty years to build my complex metal brain. I duplicated the feat in a month. Dr. Link had had to devise every step from zero. I had only to follow his beaten path. As an added factor, I work and think with a rapidity unknown to you humans. And I work twenty-four hours a day.

The time had come to test the new metal-brain. Dr. Hillory was vastly nervous. And also strangely eager. His face at times annoyed me. I could not read behind it.

I paused when the electrical cord had been attached to the neck cable of the metal-brain head, resting with eyes closed on a porcelain slab.

"I had thought of this before, of course," I informed my companion. "Making a second metal-brain. But I had reasoned that it would come to life and know the bitter loneliness I knew. I did not think of her having my companionship, and I hers."

"Hers!"

Dr. Hillory was staring at me open-mouthed.

For a moment I myself was startled. I had given myself away, and somehow, before this elderly man, I felt—embarrassed. I felt like a teen-age youngster, experiencing his first love affair. In all except the actual fact, I blushed. Metal, fortunately, does not act like the thermometer of human faces, recording human feelings.

But it was too late to hide what I meant from the canny scientist. Besides, he had to know sooner or later. I went on.

"When you stopped me at the cliff, you said why not make another robot? I had been thinking of Kay Temple at the moment. The picture of the robot that leaped into my mind, then, was not one like myself. Not mentally. The outward form would not matter. I was 'brought up' from the masculine viewpoint. This robot-mind must be given the feminine outlook."

My mechanical voice went down in tone.

"Her name will be—Eve!"

Dr. Hillory had recovered himself. "And how will you accomplish this miracle?" he said skeptically.

"Simply enough. She must be brought up in the presence of a woman. Her thought-processes, her entire outlook, will automatically be that of a woman. You must do this for me, Dr. Hillory. You are my friend. You must go to the city and see Kay Temple for me—now Mrs. Jack Hall. She is the only one who can make my plans come true. She must be the companion for Eve."

Dr. Hillory sat down, shaking his head a little dazedly. I could appreciate how he felt. Bringing a girl up here to teach a metal monster to be sweet, gentle-natured, feminine! Like trying to bring up a forest creature of lionlike build and strength to be a harmless, playful kitten. It was incongruous. Even I had my doubts. But I had equal determination.

"I suppose," he said, with a trace of the cynicism that lurked somewhere in his character, "that you will want your —Eve—to learn to giggle, like a school-girl."

I didn't answer.

Instead, I switched on the electric current. Slowly I rheostated it up, to reach the point at which electrons would drum through the iridium-sponge brain, as thoughts drum in the human mind under the forces of life. I watched, holding my breath—no, I have no breath. Sometimes I forget I am a metal man. But the idiom stands as descriptive of my feelings.

For what if the metal-brain were a failure? What if my brain was what it was by sheer accident, not the result of Dr. Link's creative genius? What if, after all, the process could not be repeated again—ever!

Loneliness. Extinction. Again my life would be wedged in maddeningly between those two words.

I held my breath, I repeat. I heard the hum of the electron-

59

discharge, coursing through the metal-brain I hoped to bring to life. And then—movement. The eyelids of the head flicked open. The brain saw. The eyelids clicked shut again, as though the brain had been startled at its sight. Then they opened and shut several more times, exactly as a human being might blink, awaking from some mysterious sleep.

"It's alive," whispered Dr. Hillory. "The brain is alive, Adam Link. We've succeeded!"

I looked down at the blinking head. The eyes seemed to look into mine, wonderingly.

"Eve!" I murmured. "My Eve!"

When we had completed the body, similar to mine but somewhat smaller, Dr. Hillory went to the city. He came back with Jack and Kay. They had come without question, immediately.

"Adam Link," Jack called as soon as he stepped from his car. "Adam, old boy! We've been wondering and worrying about you. Why did you run off like that? Why didn't you get in touch with us sooner, you tin idiot . . ."

Jack was just covering up his intense joy at seeing me, with those words. It was good to see him too, he who was my staunch friend and looked upon me more as man than robot.

Kay came up. The air seemed to hush. We stared at each other, not speaking a word.

Something inside of me turned over. My heart—as real as the "heart" with which you humans love and yearn—stopped beating. I had fled from her, but had not escaped. It was plain, now. And Kay? What was she thinking, she who had such a short time ago seen me as a man behind the illusion of metal. A man she could love . . .

Jack glanced from one to the other of us. "Say, what's the matter with you two? You're staring at each other as though you'd never met before. Kay—"

Jack of course didn't know. She had not told him; he would not understand. And my last letter to Jack had told a half-truth, that there could never be another man in Kay's life but Jack.

"Nothing, darling," Kay spoke. She took a deep breath, squeezing his arm. And then I saw how radiantly happy she was. It was an aura about her. They had been married two months. I felt a surge of joy. Kay had found herself. And I would too, soon, in a companion like myself in outward form, and like Kay inwardly.

They agreed to my plan enthusiastically.

"I take credit for the idea originally," said Jack in mock

boastfulness. "You remember once, Adam, that I suggested you make another robot, give it the feminine viewpoint, and you were automatically her lord and master."

Kay touched my arm. "I'll try to make her a girl you can be proud of, Adam."

"With you training her, that is assured," I returned, with more than mere gallantry.

"Well, let's get to work," said Dr. Hillory, impatiently. He had stood by with a look in his face that seemed to say it was all rather foolish. "You two can use my cabin," he said to Jack and Kay. "It's only a mile away."

Kay came every morning, promptly. She would turn the switch on Eve's frontal plate that brought her to life and begin her "lessons".

Eve learned to walk and talk as rapidly—within a week—as I had under Dr. Link's expert guidance. Eve, no less than myself, had a brain that learned instantly and thereafter never forgot. Once she had learned to talk, the alphabet and reading came swiftly. Then, like myself, she was given books whose contents she absorbed in page-at-a-time television scanning. She passed from "babyhood" to "schoolhood" to mental "maturity" in the span of just weeks.

The other process was not quite so simple—instilling in her growing mind the feminine viewpoint. It might take months of diligent work on Kay's part, and would take all of her time, much to Jack's ill-concealed dislike.

I had put quite a bit of thought into the matter. At last I devised an instrument that shortened the process. An aluminum helmet fitted over Kay's head, transferred her thoughts directly, over wires, to Eve. Thoughts are electrical in nature. I found the way to convert them into electrical impulses, like in a telephone. Fitted to the base of Eve's skull-piece was a vibrator whose brush-contacts touched the base of her brain. Kay's thoughts then set up an electro-vibration that modulated the electron flow of Eve's metal brain.

Electronic mind transference. Broadcast telepathy. Beamed ESP. Call it what you will. Kay's mind poured over into the receptive Eve's. I knew that Eve would then be a second Kay, a mental twin. It was Kay's mind I appreciated from the first, in an emotion as close to human love as I can reach.

Dr. Hillory and I watched developments with all the avid curiosity of the scientific mind. But I watched with more than scientific interest. We left the whole job to Kay. We seldom talked with or even went near Eve, for fear of upsetting this strange process of giving a robot a feminine mind.

Once, in fact, I was annoyed to find Dr. Hillory talking to

61

Eve. Kay had left for a moment. What he had said I don't know. I didn't want to question Eve and perhaps confuse her. But I pulled Dr. Hillory away, squeezing his arm with such force that he winced in pain.

"Keep away from her," I said bluntly.

Dr. Hillory said nothing, however. I began to wonder what to do about the scientist. But then I forgot about him, as the great moment neared, and finally arrived.

Jack, Dr. Hillory and I were in the sitting room. Kay brought Eve in, leading her by the hand. Kay had assured me, that morning, that she had done all she could. Mentally matured, Eve was as much a "woman" in outlook, as I was a "man".

I'll never forget that scene.

Outwardly, of course, Eve was just a robot, composed of bright metal, standing on stiff alloy legs, her internal mechanism making the same jingling hum that mine did. But I tried to look beyond that. Tried to see in this second intelligent robot a psychic reaction as different from mine as a human female's from a human male's. Only in that would I be satisfied.

I was Pygmalion, watching breathlessly as his ivory statue came to life.

"This is Adam Link, Eve," Kay said gravely, in our first formal introduction. "He is a wonderful man. I'm sure you'll like him."

Ridiculous? You who read do not know the solemnity of that scene, the tense expectancy behind it. Jack, Kay and Hillory, as well as myself, had become vitally interested in the problem. The future of the intelligent robot might here be at stake. We all felt that. How nearly human, and manlike and womanlike, could metal life be made?

We talked, as a group.

The conversation was general. Eve was being introduced to her first "social" gathering. I was pleased to note how reserved she was, how polite and thoughtful in the most trivial exchange of words. Gradually I became aware of her "character" and "personality". She was demure, but not meek. She was intelligent, but did not flaunt it. Deeper that than, she was sweet, loyal, sincere. She was lovely, by nature. She was—well, Kay.

"I'll be darned," Jack suddenly said, slapping his knee. "Eve, you're more Kay than Kay herself!"

It was a splendid thing for Jack to say. He had made me feel human that way too, when I first met him. He had shaken hands with me in prison, and had me play poker with the "boys". But he wasn't merely making a gallant gesture, here with Eve. He meant it. We all laughed, of course. Yes, I laughed too, inside. And I knew that Eve laughed, for she pressed her folded hands together. Kay always did that when she laughed.

Something of the tense atmosphere was relieved. Our conversation became more natural. And before we knew it, Eve and I, sitting together, were absorbedly engaged in a tete-a-tete, What would two robots talk about, you wonder? Not about electrons, rivets, gears. But about human things. She told me she liked good books, and the beauties of sunrise, and quiet moments of thought. I told her something of the world she hadn't seen.

It was then we noticed a queer phenomenon. Our conversation between ourselves gained in rapidity, like two phonographs going faster and faster. Both of us thought and spoke instantaneously. Vaguely, I noticed the others were looking at us in surprise. Our voices to them were an incoherent blur.

In the next few hours, Eve and I passed through what might have corresponded to days or weeks of human association.

Suddenly it happened.

"I love you, Adam," Eve said.

I gasped, in human terms. My first reaction was one of astonishment. And I was a little repelled. It did not seem like a mature decision, rather a mere fancy of the moment on her part. Nor did I want her to say that simply because she knew I was the only other living robot on earth. I had wanted her to say that only from the depths of her being, as human beings did when the mighty forces of love awakened.

"But Eve," I protested, speaking to her as to a child, "you hardly know me. Nor have I given you any indication that I wanted you to say such a thing."

Eve's folded hands pressed together. She was laughing.

"Adam, you poor dear," she returned. "You've been saying *you* love *me* for the past hour, in every manner short of words. I just wanted to end your suspense. I say it again, as I will to the end of time—I love you."

And in a sudden blinding moment, I knew my dream had come true. I couldn't fathom how this girl-mind worked. She was to me what women have been to men since the dawn —mystery. And in that, I knew I had succeeded.

Kay had caught on, somehow. She arose, tugging Jack by the arm. "We're not needed here any more. We're going back to the city. Dr. Hillory, you return to your cabin for a while."

Turning to us she said, smiling, "Get in touch with us soon, Adam and Eve."

And they were all three gone.

And we—the Adam and Eve of robots—looked into each other's eyes and knew that we had achieved a pinnacle of human relationship—love.

CHAPTER 9

Mechanical Zombies

A month went by. I will draw the curtain over it, as is customary in your human affairs when a man and a woman adjust themselves to a new, dual life together. For the first time, in my sojourn among humans, I knew happiness. And Eve was radiantly happy, exactly as Kay in her new-found happiness with Jack.

We went to see Dr. Hillory finally, after that golden month. It would have been a strange sight to any human eyes, I suppose. Two robots, glinting in the sunlight, strolling hand-in-hand through the woods, chatting as merrily as a country boy and girl.

A bird suddenly flew up and dashed itself against my chest plate, blinded no doubt by the shine. It fell to the ground, stunned. Eve picked it up in her steel fingers, but with all the tenderness of a soft-hearted girl, and cuddled it to her. After a moment the bird recovered, chirped uncertainly, then flew away.

Dr. Hillory's cabin was only a mile away. He eyed us with his enigmatic expression.

"How are the honeymooners?" he grinned. He seemed pleased to note how perfectly Eve—his creation and mine—had turned out.

"I've been doing a little experimenting myself," he confided. "You remember I took Kay's trans-mind helmet along. It's a fascinating gadget. I made some improvements. In fact, I eliminated the wires—made it work on the radio principle. Want to try it, Adam?"

I complied. He unhinged the skull-section next to the base of my brain and set the vibrator in contact. He had made another one, so Eve also joined the experiment.

No wires led from our two vibrators to Dr. Hillory's single helmet. Instead, a little two-masted radio aerial at its top sent out impulses that sped forth electronically.

"Do you hear me clearly, Adam Link?" came Dr. Hillory's voice in my brain. Yet his lips hadn't moved. His thought-words had directly modulated the electron-currents of my brain, reproducing the same thought-words.

"Yes," I returned, also by thought, since the system was a two-way contact. "This is rather clever but of what use—"

Dr. Hillory's mental voice burst in. "Adam, strike Eve on the frontal-plate with your fist."

To my surprise, I instantly balled my fingers and clanged my metal fist against Eve's frontal plate. It didn't hurt her, of course. But Eve did a strange thing. With a short, frightened cry, she reached her hands behind her head, to rip the vibrator away.

"Stop, Eve!" commanded Dr. Hillory. "Put your hands down. Fold them in your lap."

She did. And she did not press them together; she wasn't laughing. I sensed that she was instead very, very frightened. As for myself, up till this moment, I was little more than startled at Dr. Hillory's commands, and his strange game with us.

"Adam!" Eve cried. "Don't you see? We're in his power—"

Lightning struck my brain. Instinctively I also raised my hands to rip away the little instrument that gave him such command over us.

"Stop, Adam! Put *your* hands in your lap."

I fought. I strained with every steel muscle. But my machine's strength meant nothing. My hands dropped obediently.

Dr. Hillory was looking at us triumphantly. I had long suspected he was not a man to be trusted. Now he had revealed himself.

"Adam Link," he said gratingly, "your brain controls every cable and cog in your body. But your brain, in turn, is under *my* control. I am amazed at my own success. Obviously a command given by me, impinging on your electron-currents, is tantamount to a command given by yourself. Perhaps you can explain it better than I. But this is certain—I can do with you as I will."

I tried speaking and found I could, as long as he had made no direct command against it.

"Let us free, Dr. Hillory. You have no right to keep up this control. We are minds, like yourself, with the right of liberty."

Dr. Hillory shook his head slowly. "No, Adam. You will stay under my domination—"

It was then I acted—or tried to. I tried to leap at him. A swift mental command from him—and I stopped short. Fighting an intangible force—fighting my own brain—I strained to move on. Every muscle cable was taut. Every wheel in my body meshed for movement. Electrical energy lay ready to spring forth in a powerful flood. But the mental command

66

did not come from my brain. Instead, slowly, my body inched back and finally eased with a grind of unlocking gears.

Hillory had won.

He stood before me, my master. I had the strength of ten men in one arm, the power of a mighty engine at my fingertips. I could have taken, in three seconds, his puny, soft body and torn it to bloody shreds. Yet there he stood, my master.

Hillory eased his caught breath, as though not sure himself till then that he could stop me. Color came back into his face.

You're my slave," he said, "And I have plans—"

Eve and I looked at each other helplessly. A sadness radiated from Eve's eyes. Our happiness shattered suddenly like a fragile soap-bubble.

If I had any hope of breaking from Hillory's clutch, it was quickly dispelled. First he made us lie down, then removed our frontal-plates. It was simple for him to unhook the cables from the batteries that gave us life. We blinked out of consciousness.

When we regained our senses—it was like a dreamless sleep —we realized our true hopelessness. Hillory had welded the vibrators to the backs of our skull-pieces so firmly that it would be impossible for us to tear them away with our fingers. Secondly, he had installed turn-off switches in the battery-circuit, so that we could be turned off when he desired. Eve's switch had been removed before, when she reached "maturity". Now it was back, this means of "turning off" our life.

"While I wear the helmet, you are under my command," the scientist said matter-of-factly. "Whenever I wish to take the helmet off, I simply turn you two off first. You cannot escape me, and you must do as I wish."

In the following month, part of his plan unfolded. He forced me to devise a new and larger robot body. When the parts came, from factories, my fingers put them together, under his command.

Completed, the body stood eight feet high, without a head. It was a super-powerful mechanism, with muscle cables and cogs all proportionately larger than mine. Twice as much electrical power would be needed to run it. It was probably the upper limit in robot bodies, within the boundaries of flexibility, mobility and strength. Anything larger would have been clumsy. Anything stronger would have been too heavy to walk without sinking into the ground.

Dr. Link had built my body as nearly in human proportion as possible. I stood five feet ten inches and weighed 500 pounds. This robot body was two feet higher and weighed 900 pounds. And when Hillory finally revealed his purpose, I screamed in protest.

67

"Put Eve's head on that robot body," he had commanded.

"No!" I bellowed. "What monstrous motive have you behind all this—"

He let me rage on for a while. He did that once in a while, playing with me cat and mouse, knowing he had the upper hand. Eve pulled at my arm. "Please don't, dear!" she begged. "It's no use!"

And it was no use. I quieted. Eve was turned off. Though it revolted me in every atom of my being, I unfastened her headpiece gently and attached it to the new body. I trembled doing it. Trembled with anguish. Though changing bodies does not mean so much to a robot as it would to a human being, it is nevertheless a disagreeable thought. I had come to love every contour, every dent and scratch on Eve's former body. She would be strange to me, in the new one.

Finally every little wire had been connected, between her brain and the relay switches in the body's neck. Then I bolted the neck-piece in place, holding the head firmly. At the last, under Hillory's command, I snapped the on-switch.

With a creak and groan of new metal, the body arose. It towered above us both like a Goliath. I shed mental tears, and I could see the same in Eve's eyes as she looked down at me. This was as agonizing to us as to a human wife suddenly finding herself three feet taller than her husband. It was monstrous.

Hillory was ignoring our feelings, in this as in all previous things. Hopelessly, I tried to appeal to him.

"She's my mental mate," I said, "Don't you understand? She's my—wife. We have feelings. Please—"

The scientist laughed.

"Metal beings, parading as humans," he spat out. "You, Adam, prating about loneliness, wanting a companion, mental love! It was sickening the day you and Eve talked of loving each other. That's all sentimental, twisted rot. Even among humans. You two, in the first place, are just metal beings. You have no rights alongside humans. You were created by human hands. I'll show the world how to really use robots—as *clever instruments.*"

Instruments of what? What had he meant?

We soon found out. That very day, Hillory tested the range of his remote-control over Eve by radio. Eve, astride her new giant body, was sent step by step away, till she vanished in the woods. Still the scientist commanded her to move on, watching an instrument that recorded distance and control. Altogether, Eve was sent a mile, and came back obediently.

At no time, obviously, had she felt the slightest weakening

68

of Hillory's remote-control impulses, borne by high-frequency radio-waves. And radio-waves had a limitless range.

"You can be sent down to the city," Hillory remarked, pleased with the results. "Under my control, you can be made to do anything I want there."

"What are you planning, you devil?" I demanded.

A sly leer was my only answer.

That night, Eve was sent down the mountains to the city. Hillory was able to guide her easily enough, though she had never been there before. His mental commands told her every step. Conversely, her sharp comprehensive thoughts came back to him, whenever she was in doubt as to a road or turn. When she reached the city, in the dead of the night, Hillory read street signs through her and directed her footsteps. Svengali had never had the full, diabolical control over his Trilby that Hillory had over Eve.

At times, though the streets of the small city were nearly deserted at this hour, late wanderers spied the tall alien form. Eve involuntarily informed Hillory, and he would cause her to duck into shadowed doorways, or down alleys.

"This is perfect," exulted Hillory to me. "I'm really there, by proxy. Through Eve, I can accomplish any deed within reason, without stirring a step from here."

Eventually, Eve informed Hillory that she stood before a bank. Hillory sent her to the back entrance, and after a guarded look around, told her to shoulder down the door without making unnecessary noise. Inside, her keen mechanical eyesight picked her way to the vault. It was not a particularly sturdy vault. The bank was a small one.

Hillory gave an amazing order.

I heard all this through my mental contact with Hillory's helmet. He told Eve to pull open the vault door. Through Eve's involuntary thoughts, we could almost picture her tugging at the heavy metal door. Finally she braced her feet. The stupendous strength of her giant steel body exerted itself in one furious tug. There must have been a terrific grind of strained, breaking metal, as the vault lock cracked apart. Eve's great new hands had done a job that might have balked a blast of nitroglycerine.

Eve did not know what money was, but Hillory did. He had her stuff great packets of bills in a sack and hurry out. The whole episode was over in three minutes. Eve arrived back without mishap, the sack dangling over her shoulder.

Hillory had robbed a bank, without the slightest personal danger. Was that his purpose, to amass ill-gotten wealth? He read my thought.

"No, Adam," he said suavely. "This is a matter of personal

69

revenge. The President of the bank once refused me a loan."

That made his motive still more petty and unworthy. I looked at poor Eve. Her eyes were haunted. She knew she had been forced to do something wrong. Her Kay-mind told her that. She was miserable. But I was more miserable. I had brought her to life. I had not dashed myself to pieces, there at the cliff. On my soul—robot or not—rested the deed.

I tried to remonstrate with Hillory. He clicked us off, laughing, with little more regard for us than he would have had for cleverly trained dogs.

The following day, Hillory tuned the radio to the city's station. The news blared forth—

The Midcity Bank was mysteriously robbed last night. The thief or thieves broke down the back door and raided the vault, escaping with $20,000. The vault door did not seem to be blown down. It had apparently been forced open by some amazingly powerful lever or instrument. Police are puzzled.

They are investigating strange reports that a robot form was seen last night by several people, described as a huge one ten feet tall. Is it Adam Link, the intelligent robot, with a new body? Has he returned, after five months of mysterious absence, to commit this deed? Before he left, Adam Link was accepted almost with human status. Has he returned now to vindicate those who said he was a Frankenstein monster, dangerous to human life and property?

Frankenstein! Again that hideous allusion was springing up about me after I had labored so hard to erase it in the minds of humans.

"You are ruining all my past efforts," I accused Hillory. "I saved life, helped humans, showed that the intelligent robot would do good, not harm. Now, you are destroying that—"

"Nothing of the sort," retorted Hillory evenly. "I have reasoned the matter out carefully. After perfecting my robot-control, and doing one or two other personal things, I'll take my plans to big business interests in New York. The few little things that happen here won't matter. I'll sell you as a great new invention."

He might have been speaking of a new type of radio, or automobile.

I tried to speak slowly, calmly, in answer.

"You are making a frightful mistake, Hillory. When I came to life, and lived in the world awhile, I saw the enormous difficulties of introducing robot-life. I saw from my own experiences that it would not be like introducing a new mechanical gadget. For I have a mind and feelings and human emotions. Human life is complicated enough, without adding another complex factor. Before the cliff there, I had made up

70

my mind it was better for the secret of the metal-brain to vanish. Both for my sake and the world's. Foolishly, I let the thought of a companion robot sway me to stay in life. Yet perhaps the problem is not insoluble. But I tell you this, Dr. Hillory—I and I alone must decide. I alone, the Adam of intelligent robots, can find a way to introduce robot-life without creating future disaster."

Hillory hardly heard.

"Rubbish! Your whole approach has been wrong. Who are you to tell humans what is best for them? You're no more than a clever mechanical toy, with pseudo-human reactions. I have figured out the way to introduce robots. Not as independent individuals who wander around in a half-human daze, looking for mental love. But as an organized, controlled force of workers, under the strict domination of their human creators and masters. As for your so-called 'feelings', they are spurious. Like a phonograph, you have learned to imitate the human things. You are no more than a clever mechanism."

He looked at Eve and me as one might look at a piece of prized furniture.

"We are life," I said doggedly. I wished at that moment that my metallic larynx did not sound so cold, so expressionless. It destroyed the meaning of my words. "Life is in the mind. We have minds. Dr. Link realized that. You must too—"

"Shut up!" roared Hillory in exasperation. "Why should I listen to your meaningless drivel?"

I was helpless to go on. He had commanded me to stop talking. He was master of every atom of my body. Eve and I looked at each other. She understood. The future of robots lay in my hands. But I was a pawn in Hillory's hands. The dread thought loomed before us—what would be the fate of our future kind? Of the robot—*race?* Slavery! We must have felt then like the Adam and Eve of Biblical history, denied Eden, foreseeing only misery and suffering for their people.

Hillory sent Eve out again the next night. His sly look told of some other hideous deed in mind.

A short time later, a car's motor and brakes sounded outside, and then its horn. Hillory glanced out of the window.

"Kay!" he breathed. But he seemed prepared.

Kay rushed in. She was alone. She glanced at us both.

"Adam!" she cried. "I had to come. Is there anything wrong? Where's Eve?"

"No, there is nothing wrong, Kay," I returned, but the words had been projected from Hillory's mind. I had no power to stop them, or utter words of my own. "Eve is all right. She just went out for a walk."

Kay heaved a tremulous sigh.

71

"Then all those ugly rumors are groundless, just as Jack said." Her voice held deep relief. "The robbery naturally would be pinned on Adam Link, Jack said. People are like that. He said the criminals probably did things in such a way as to leave signs pointing to you. You're their perfect cover-up. I wanted to come up yesterday, but Jack said not to disturb you and Eve until you called for us. But I was so worried that tonight I jumped in the car and came up, just to make sure everything is all right."

There was still a trace of doubt in her voice. She was staring at Hillory, and the queer helmet he wore.

"Adam and I were just finishing a little experiment," Hillory said easily.

Kay turned to me again. "Then everything *is* all right?"

"Of course, Kay. It was nice of you to be concerned and come up, but why not come back some other time, when we aren't so busy?"

Hillory's words, of course, through my helpless brain and larynx by proxy. I strained to put in a note of warning, distress. But a robot's voice is devoid of human emotion.

But strangely, instead of taking the hint to go, she seemed curious over the experiment. She moved toward the control board of the helmet, connected to it by wires.

"This looks something like the helmet I used with Eve," she said.

I could see Hillory's impatience for her to go. But he could not afford to arouse her suspicions. He began to describe the experiment in general, meaningless terms.

Suddenly Kay moved.

She moved with a swiftness and purpose that startled us both. Her hand grasped the switch cutting off current to the helmet. Hillory recovered and clutched at her wrist. With a furious effort, Kay opened the switch.

That was all that was needed.

CHAPTER 10

Machine Battles Machine

The helmet went dead. I was no longer in Hillory's mental control. In two bounds I was before him. I grabbed the helmet from his head and flung it to the floor. Then I grasped his two shoulders in a vise-like grip and held him. I think if my face had shown any expression at that moment, I would have been grinning—but with no trace of humor.

Hillory's face had gone dead-white in fear. He squirmed and moaned in my adamant clutch, expecting immediate death.

Let me make a confession at this moment. For one split instant, with rage shaking every cell of my iridium-sponge brain, I thought of tearing Hillory's head from his body. But only for an unguarded instant. Then reason came to me. A robot must never kill a human of his own free will. It was a thing I would never do.

I merely held Hillory firmly. To Kay I said: "Thanks, Kay. You've saved me—"

"I knew there was something wrong!" Her lips were quivering now, in reaction to the excitement. "I knew it couldn't be you, Adam, that told me to go so brusquely. And Dr. Hillory is a poor actor." And Kay, I reflected, was an intelligent girl.

"What is this all about? What horrible—" Kay seemed about to go to pieces.

"Buck up," I snapped. I told the story briefly. Then I instructed her to get a bottle of acid and apply it to the instrument welded on my skull-piece. A few minutes later the vibrator fell away. I was free entirely of the helmet control.

Not till then did I release Hillory. He staggered to a chair, mute and mortally frightened. The man who had been my master sat there now, a cowering wretch.

"Hillory—" I began.

There was an interruption outside. The clank of metal feet sounded. Through the open door I could see Eve's body, glinting in moonlight. She had come back, also released from the mental control. She stood beside Kay's car, swaying on her feet, as though utterly dazed and lost.

I ran out.

"Eve!" I yelled. "We're free. Eve, dear—"

73

I suppose I felt at that moment as any man would, when he and his loved one are reunited after a deadly peril. I extended my hand.

Eve took it with a glad cry.

And then suddenly she yanked at my arm, throwing me to the ground. For an agonized moment I thought she had gone mad. Then, as her great body came at me I realized what had happened.

I leaped to my feet. A glance over my shoulder told me the situation. I saw within the open, lighted doorway of the cabin. Like a fool, I had forgotten about Hillory. He had picked up the helmet, turned on the power, and was fighting Kay off. Brutally, he crashed his fist against her chin and the girl toppled to the floor, knocked cold.

Hillory had no more control over me. But he did have over Eve.

Her great body came at me, under Hillory's command. Its mighty arms clutched for me, grabbed me, squeezed with machine-given power. My frontal plates groaned. I squirmed loose somehow, and staggered back. A stunning blow from Eve's powerful hand caught me at the side of the head. My left tympanum went dead, ruptured. I reeled.

"Eve!" I shouted. "Eve—don't!"

But of course it was no use. It was not Eve who was attacking me. It was Hillory. And there we fought, Eve and I, two beings who loved each other but who were battling with the fury of giants. Eve was fighting to destroy me. I was fighting for my life.

I knew quickly that I had no chance. Eve's body was almost twice as heavy and powerful. I was slightly quicker in movement, and that alone saved me from almost instant destruction.

Mighty blows from her great fists thundered against my body. My return blows fell short. I danced out of her grasp. Those arms had crushing strength. I tried to flee. In three mighty strides Eve had caught up, knocked me off my feet. A powerful leg rained kicks at my fallen form, denting metal and endangering delicate mechanisms within. Then, the great form jumped on me. Nine hundred pounds crashed down on my chest. It was very nearly the fatal blow.

But I managed to roll aside, escaping the second such stroke, aimed at my head. Hillory wanted my brain crushed. He wanted to destroy me utterly, and have Eve left under his control.

The battle could not last much longer. Within seconds I would be crushed, broken, lifeless.

I did the only thing left. I ran—but this time to the cliff

edge, where I had once nearly invited death. Eve's hands clutched at me, and then drew back. Hillory was willing to let me plunge over the cliff, and meet destruction five hundred feet below. I went over, dropping like a stone. . . .

The fall seemed interminable.

It is said that you humans, when falling or drowning, see your whole life before your mind. I saw mine—not once but a hundred times. Every detail stood out with stark clarity. But one livid thing stood out above all others—the thought of Eve, my beloved creation, remaining alive in the hands of a human fiend . . .

Yet one part of my brain, as I fell, was cool and calculating. It kept track of my descent, counting off the feet and yards by that automatic sense of timing and measurement which is part of me.

A hundred feet to the ground it announced, and then acted. It made my arms and legs flail, shifting my center of gravity. My body had turned head over heels four times in falling. But when I landed, it was squarely on my feet. To have landed on my head would have been immediate destruction.

I have instant reflexes. The moment my feet-plates touched ground, my leg-cables flexed, taking up as much of the shock as possible. It might be the margin to save me. The rest was a clash of grinding, bending, breaking metal that horrified my own ear. I had fallen on a patch of grassy ground, but with the force of a motorcycle hitting a stone wall at 300 miles an hour.

My mind swam out of a blur. One eye was wrecked and useless, but with the other I looked over my body. My legs were twisted, crumpled lumps that had been driven up into my pelvic region. One arm was broken completely off and lay twenty feet away. My frontal plates had split in half and now stuck half-way over my sunken head. Every cog, wire and wheel below my shoulders was scattered around in an area of more than fifty feet.

But I lived! I lived!

My brain was whole, though badly jolted. By a miracle, the battery cable to my head was intact. The battery was cracked, but working. I could move one arm slightly. I was little more than a battery, head and arm, but I lived!

And thus I had played out my one slim chance. I had thrown myself over the cliff—but not as a suicide. I had hoped this miracle would happen. Up above, Hillory must be looking down. He must be seeing the faint patch of metal shining in the moonlight, unmoving. He would be certain of my utter destruction.

Perhaps now he would be turning away, ordering Eve inside. And there plotting his scheme of bringing to life a horde of mind-enslaved robots.

But I lived. . . .

I began crawling. Little more than a head, battery and arm, I began crawling along. The stump of my arm dug into the soil, flexed, and moved me an inch at a time. Behind me trailed shreds and tags of metal, all that was left of my body. My steel backbone, to which was attached the battery case, head and arm, moved as a unit, but the rest was shreds. Hour after hour I crawled along, like some strange half-mangled slug that clung to life.

Yes, I knew agony. The shattering of my body meant nothing, but my brain itself ached. Some few crushed cells were warping my electron-currents, creating a sort of hammering static. It throbbed like the beat of a great hammer. I do not know what your human pain is. But I would have gladly exchanged any possible form of it for the crashes and thuds within my brain that seemed like the sledge-blows of a giant.

But worse than that "physical" agony was my mental torment.

What if the twisted cables and gears of my arm failed? What if the battery cracked wide open? What if a little bolt or wire slipped out of place? At any moment it might happen. And I would lie there, dead. Or paralyzed, awaiting death. And up there in my cabin-laboratory, Hillory, and poor Eve . . .

But metal is sturdy. And Dr. Link had built my body with care. I crawled all that night and the next day, through woods, meadows, and stretches of boulder-strewn land. I knew where I was going, if I could get there. Once, reaching a brook, it took me an hour to figure a crossing. I could not risk water for fear of a short-circuit. I nudged a log into the stream. It caught against rocks. I crawled across.

But I will not go into the nightmarish detail of that journey. Forty-eight hours later, again at night, I had crawled five miles. Before me lay a farmhouse, the nearest one, as I had known, to my hideaway. It had a telephone.

I reached the back door. Luckily, as with many unmolested farmer folk, it was unlocked. I made my way in and found the telephone, but it was on the wall out of my stunted reach. Working as soundlessly as I could, I pulled a chair over. From that perch, I was barely able to reach the phone. It was the old-fashioned hand-ringing type, still prevalent in that region.

With my one good hand I lifted the receiver, left it dangling, and rang the bell. A sleepy operator answered. I hurriedly gave the long-distance number in the city nearby. Jack's number.

I heard the ringing of the phone at the other end. I also

76

heard a stir from one of the other rooms. Jack answered at the same time that a burly farmer appeared, snapping on the lights.

"Jack!" I yelled. "It's Adam Link. Come and get me. Trace this call—"

That was all I had time for. The farmer blazed away at me with a shotgun he carried. The first shot wrecked my arm swivel, making me completely helpless. The second, by its concussion, tumbled me from my perch. I fell to the floor with a clatter and lay still. The farmer did not know what he had shot at, in those ghastly seconds, whether beast or nameless thing. He shut himself up in the next room, then, with his wailing family. I will never know what he thought of the whole thing.

Jack arrived within an hour, in his car, and took me away, explaining to the farmer as incoherently as the farmer stammered his story. In the car were Kay and Tom Link.

Kay wept unashamedly.

"Adam! You're alive—thank God."

I told my story briefly. Kay told hers. Hillory had released her of course, after I was gone, afraid of a kidnapping charge. Kay had returned to the city. In a red rage at Hillory, Jack had driven to his place the next day—yesterday. He had not met Hillory, only the menacing form of Eve, who waved for him to leave. Hillory spoke, through Eve, saying he was preparing papers for patent rights on the helmet-control of robots.

Back in the city, Jack had called Tom, who came by plane from his law office. They had been discussing, when I phoned, some legal way to forestall Hillory.

Tom Link, my "cousin", looked at me sadly.

"Meeting you this way hurts, Adam," he said sincerely. "I didn't know you were in trouble." My last letter to him had not revealed my hideaway or purpose.

He went on grimly. "We must stop Hillory some way. We can try to pin the robbery on him, with yourself as chief witness. You have legal status since your trial, Adam. Failing that, we can contest the patent or file counter-patent or. . . ."

Tom was vague, uncertain. It was a tricky situation. "The trouble is," he burst out, continuing, "that you are still not a true citizen, Adam. As I've written you at times, I have your application papers on file in Washington, but nothing has come of it. Red tape, of course. If only you were a citizen under federal law, Hillory would not dare talk of *patenting* you, like a common machine. The infernal nerve of him. Yet, he might succeed."

Yes, that was the rub. As Adam Link, United States Citizen, no scheming wretch like Hillory could do this to me. But as plain Adam Link, robot machine, I had no defense against such tactics.

Adam Link, citizen. Had events again closed that door to me, forever?

Tom raved on some more, but I broke in. I think my voice must have startled them. Perhaps for once something of the burning emotion I felt was reflected in my dead, phonic voice.

"Vengeance," I said, "is mine."

Three days later, working day and night at an accelerated, driving pace, I had a new body. I was in Dr. Link's old workshop, my "birthplace". Tom had locked the place without removing its contents, for sentimental reasons. I had been created here, over a year before. Now a new Adam Link was replacing the old.

My new body was eight feet tall, excluding a head. Bringing me only as a living head, Tom and Jack had, under my instructions, connected me to a broken, partly dismantled robot body Dr. Link had first made for me, then discarded as not quite what he wanted. Working with this basis, I rebuilt the body piece by piece, strengthening, improving, employing greatly advanced mechanical principles.

At last it was done, and I prepared to leave.

Kay, Jack and Tom wore solemn faces. Within, I was solemn too. I knew what I had to do.

"I'll bring Hillory down alive," I promised grimly. "But before that—" I could not finish the thought.

Kay burst into tears. She loved Eve too.

I left. I had told them to come up, with police, if I did not return in twenty-four hours. Hillory could be arrested for living on my property, already signed over to Jack and Kay. Perhaps then they might win a legal victory over him.

I was there at dawn. If I had thought to surprise Hillory asleep, I saw my mistake. Eve's form, sitting before the cabin, rose up mechanically, with a shout of alarm. Hillory had somehow rigged her up as a sentry.

The cabin door flew open and Hillory's bald head peered out. He saw me running up as fast as I could. His eyes popped. I must have seemed to him like a ghost from the dead—a robot's vengeful ghost.

But he darted back in, obviously to his helmet-control, and Eve's great form lumbered out to meet me. This I knew was inevitable, that I would have to battle Eve again.

"You escaped death somehow, Adam Link," Eve's voice said. But I knew it was Hillory talking, through her. I had no way of telling whether he was perturbed or not. "I'll smash you completely this time, before my eyes," he concluded defiantly.

I stopped ten feet before Eve's crouching, waiting form. "Eve, listen. I know you can hear and understand." I went on rapidly. "I have to battle you, perhaps kill you. It is the only way. I must destroy you if I can, so that Hillory does not destroy me. Hillory must not be allowed to introduce robot-slaves. This is all torture to you, darling, I know. You are fighting me when you don't want to. And I will be bent on your destruction—even, if necessary, that of your brain. Your life! I love you, Eve. Forgive me—"

"Love!" scoffed the robot before me. For a moment I thought it was Eve. Then I knew it was Hillory, hearing my words, and mocking. "Mechanical puppets, both of you."

And then we were battling.

How can I describe that battle? A struggle between two metal titans, each with the ruthless machine-powered strength of dozens of men? It seemed unreal even to me.

We came together with a clang that resounded through the still mountain air like a cannon's roar. We locked arms, straining to throw each other. But now I was no longer at a disadvantage. We were equally matched. Two robots constructed for maximum power, speed and endurance. Unyielding metal against unyielding metal.

We looked into each other's eyes, told each other that though our bodies fought, our minds loved.

We broke apart. We came at each other with swinging arms. Mailed fists clanked against our adamant armors. The blows would have broken the back of an elephant. Within us, gears, cogs and wheels clashed in spurts and reverses as we weaved and danced around like boxers in a ring. We did not move as agilely as human boxers, however. The robot body must ever be inferior, in sheer efficiency, to nature's organic robots.

Suddenly my adversary—I no longer thought of her as Eve, but Hillory—stepped back, stooping. He shot forward in a football tackle, toppling me backward. Then, while I lay slightly stunned, he picked me up by heel and arm, and flung me over his head. I landed with a metallic crash. The next second a huge boulder whizzed past my head. Then another . . . but I was dodging.

I was on my knees when he came at me, hammering at my skull-piece with his ponderous arms. I flung my arms up in protection. He sought to destroy my brain. Once that was crushed, my powerful body was senseless junk.

I lunged forward at his knees, hurling him to the ground with a thunderous crash. I had my chance then—a perfect chance to stamp my iron heel down on the head, crunching it. But I didn't.

Eve's eyes stared at me.

The chance passed, as my enemy rolled away, swung erect. But I had been a fool. One blow and Eve would have known non-existence. It would have been sheer mercy, to save her from a living death. If the chance came again, I would not hesitate. . . .

I hardly know what went on in the following minutes. Once my enemy picked up a boulder that ten men could not have budged and hurled it at me like a bomb. I dodged but it scraped my side, tearing three rivets loose. Again, he locked his arms around me from the back and crunched them together so fiercely that metal screamed. But I heaved him over my back, breaking the hold.

We fought on, like two mad giants. Our colossal blows at one another would have felled the largest dinosaur of Earth's savage past. Our mechanical apparatus within began to feel the repeated shock. Parts were being strained to the breaking point. It couldn't go on forever. One of us would break down.

I had a dim hope that my enemy would succumb first. Hillory had had to fight by proxy, from a distance. I had fought from a closer range. I had gotten more telling blows in. His inner mechanisms had received the most terrific jolting. It was his second battle. I had punched at the head as often as I could, jarring the brain within—even though it was Eve's.

I cannot describe the hollow ache that came with the thought of winning by killing Eve. But I had to win. I had to save the future robot race from slavery. And the human race, beyond that, from the eventual catastrophe of such a murderous course.

I aimed another blow, straight for what would be the human jaw.

Suddenly it was over.

The other robot's arms dropped. There was a stunned, dazed air about the whole body. It swayed a moment, then its knee swivels bent and it crashed to the ground. It lay sprawled, eyes closed.

For a long moment I stared. I heard no sound from the other body. It lay utterly rigid, quiet. And then I realized it was dead. The brain had died first. My final blow had killed Eve. . . .

I stood looking down at the battered wreck. I looked beyond it. I could almost see a body like Kay's lying there, a human body, the real Eve. Her eyes were closed. Perhaps there was a peaceful smile on the lips.

I turned slowly.

Slowly, my steps dragging, I strode for the cabin, to confront the man who had killed my Eve. The man who considered us nothnig more than mechanical puppets, with which he could play as he desired.

Hillory darted out of the door. His face was a ghastly white. I clutched at him, caught his coat, but he tore loose. He ran, as though from some monster. And at that moment, I *was* a monster. I pounded after him. What things I screeched, I do not know.

He ran past the edge of the cliff, taking the shortest course to the road. Abruptly a great piece of the cliff-edge parted from its matrix. The stupendous vibrations of the previous battle had loosened the piece. It plunged below. Hillory was on it.

I dug my foot-plates into the soil and leaned backward, barely halting at the edge of the fissure. I looked down. I saw the white dot of Hillory's body land. I knew he hadn't survived the fall, as I had.

CHAPTER 11

Sherlock of Steel

Then I went back, staring at Eve's dead body. She was gone, my mate. I was alive. Why did it have to turn out this way, I groaned mentally. Why had it not ended for me too? There might not be a Heaven for robots. But there was a Hell—earth.

It had begun to rain. I knelt motionless beside Eve's broken form. There would have to be a funeral, burial, all that. Kay and Jack Hall found me that way when they arrived. Police were with them.

"Adam!" Jack yelled. "Hillory is dead. We saw him plunge over the cliff. Your troubles are over."

"Over?" I echoed hollowly, staring at Eve. "Yes, it's over —for Eve."

I started. I heard a moan. A raspy, metallic sound. It came from Eve's microphonic throat.

"You poor fool," Jack said witheringly. "Did you think she was dead? Haven't you heard of someone being *knocked cold?* She's coming to."

"Adam—" One of her hands reached for mine. It was all she could say in her joy. I couldn't say anything.

"Just a minute!"

The police captain stepped forward. "I have a warrant for the arrest of Adam Link, for the robbery of Midcity Bank."

Jack whirled. "But Dr. Hillory caused that. You see, Hillory used remote-control radio and had Adam and Eve Link in his power. He is the true robber."

The police officer was terse. "Sorry, I'm following orders. Evidence shows that a robot did the crime. Adam Link must come with me."

"But it wasn't Adam Link," Tom spoke up suddenly. "It was Eve Link."

"No, it was me," I snapped quickly. I didn't want Eve to go through all the turmoil of a court trial and face possible sentence, if worst came to worst. I sent an angry glance at Tom Link, trying to shut him up.

"Eve, I say," Tom insisted.

"I'll have to take them both along," said the captain. He

and his men were faintly smiling. The whole thing, I could see, struck them as queerly humorous. One robot trying to "shield" another, like humans might. Only Jack and Kay and Tom really understood.

But I noticed that behind their smiles, the police were tense, ready to grab for their pistols. We were fearsome metal monsters nine feet tall, with our former heads attached to our new bodies. I could see that inevitable thought coursing through their minds—*Frankenstein!*

No use to resist, of course. It would have been easy—Eve and I rushing through them and laughing at their guns. Yes, but then what? Hounded, persecuted. State militia called as a last resort. No, that was the last thing in the world I would do. I had patterned my life in the human way. We would face the agencies of law, though I hated the thought of again going through its legal mazes.

"Come, Eve," I said quietly. "We must deal with humans on their own footing."

We were taken down the mountain road to the city in the two squad cars. The engines groaned wth our separate weights of nearly a half-ton each. Jack, Kay and Tom followed in their car.

Before the indictment a few hours later, Tom managed to whisper to me.

"Don't shield Eve, Adam. Let her go through the trial. She will then acquire human status, as you did in yours. I'm certain I can save her from the charges—but only with you as witness of Hillory's evil control. You are a 'person' in court records. Therefore your testimony will be official."

I nodded. Tom's clear legal reasoning had foreseen all that. My thoughts leaped ahead. Eve exonerated, legally a "human". Then both of us would apply for citizenship, as my creator, Dr. Link, had visioned from the first day of my "birth". And even—my heart sang—a church wedding for Eve and me. Why not? Then we would be the moral equals of humans in the eyes of the world.

The words of the official reading the indictment crashed into my thoughts.

"Eve Link is hereby accused of the robbery of Midcity Bank, and of the murders of John Deering, Tony Pucelli, and Hans Unger, all of this city."

Tom started. *"What?"* he demanded. "Why is Eve Link being accused of three *murders?"*

The official looked up with hard cynicism.

"Investigation reports just came in, before we drew up the final indictment. The next night, after the bank robbery, those three men were murdered—Deering, Pucelli and Unger. In

83

each case, clues pointed to a robot. Marks on their bodies could only have been made by a metal instrument. Even bits of metal filing were found."

Jack groaned, at my side.

"I get it. You remember how the papers played up the robot angle immediately after the robbery. Everybody read it the next morning. Some clever criminal organization in the city, seeing that, promptly carried out three gang murders the next night. Using metal clubs and leaving metal filings as obvious clues, it all points to Eve as the culprit. She was *framed*."

Tom groaned, too. "How clever. How dammably clever."

The official shrugged. "You'll have to prove your claims in court. The trial will be held in a month."

Tom turned a pale face to me. He didn't have to say it. *Eve was doomed.*

Frankenstein! Frankenstein! Already I could hear the word shrieking through the city, in every newspaper and from every radio speaker. Eve had the noose around her neck.

Jack put a hand on my arm. I think I was trembling. When my thoughts are disorganized, my internal machinery is also.

"We'll put detectives on the job," Jack said. "We have a month's time—" But he exchanged a hopeless glance with Tom.

Detectives. A month's time. A clever criminal ring that had covered up its trail cunningly. A whole city aroused against the robots parading as humans, taking life in secret. It added up to zero—for Eve. My thoughts crashed to that conclusion in seconds.

I warned Tom and Jack to say no more. I turned to Eve.

"Go to your cell. They will lock you in. On no account must you try to leave." I paused. "We must accept what comes. The case is hopeless, Do you understand, dear?"

Eve was shocked. I could detect that in the way her internal hum had missed a moment, exactly as a human heart may skip. She had been waiting for one word of hope from me. I gave her none. She was led away in a dead silence.

"I'll visit her every day," Kay said sympathetically. "Poor child, she'll feel so frightened and alone." She glanced at me almost contemptuously for my brutal dismissal.

"Drive to my mountain cabin-laboratory," I directed, when we were outside.

"Out with it," Jack demanded shrewdly. "Something's seething in that brain of yours."

"I thought you were a man, Adam Link," Kay said furiously. "A man who would fight for one he loves. You could at least have said one word of encouragement. Why did you tell Eve that the case was hopeless?"

I winced a little under her scorn. But I spoke firmly. "For the benefit of the officials. And the reporters waiting for the least little rumor or report to play up. And most important, for the benefit, eventually, of the criminal ring dumping their murders in Eve's lap. They'll sit back now, confident that we won't try a thing. They won't know that a detective is on the case. A detective by the name of—Adam Link."

They gasped.

"*You?*" Jack snapped.

"Yes, why not? Without meaning to boast, I think quicker than any human. I have super-keen ears and eyes. I have strength and quickness and powers no human detective has. I can do more in a month than ten men."

Jack shook his head sadly. "You've forgotten one thing, Adam. You've naturally come to think of yourself as human. But the whole meaning of the word detective is spying in secret. How can you do that—with your metal body?"

I left the question unanswered till we had reached my place. Then I stepped to my workbench and brought back a bowl of sticky, rubbery plastic. "I was working on this before Hillory upset my plans. I was toying with the idea of—well, look—"

I smeared some of the plastic over my frontal-plate with a spatula. It was opaque, hiding the metal. Its color was that of human flesh.

"My disguise," I said. "Human disguise."

The three of them stared at me, wonderingly. "You might just be able to work a miracle," said Kay finally.

Yes, it would almost have to be a miracle at that. Tom might prove Hillory's actual guilt in the case of mere robbery. But three human lives had also been allegedly taken, cold-bloodedly, by the Frankenstein monster named Eve Link. That was what we were up against.

I turned to the thought-helmet, the one with which Hillory had diabolically controlled Eve. Now there would be at least one benefit from the hell we had been through. The thought-helmets were a godsend in this hour of need.

Switching on the power, I sent a radio-beam searching for Eve's mind. My electrical thoughts modulated the beam, in a process akin to telepathy.

"Eve," I called silently. "Can you hear me?"

"Adam!" came back almost instantly over the two-way conducting beam. "I've been so afraid—"

"Don't be, darling," I soothed. "And forgive me for leaving you so coldly. It was necessary. I'm going to save you, Eve. I'm going to save you. I promise."

But it was not till two precious weeks later that I began. I had had to work day and night, perfecting the plastic, giving it the rubbery consistency of human flesh. And also making it adhere firmly to metal. I think a human chemist would not have solved the problem in a year. But I was driven by a demon. Every tick of my internal electrical distributor counted off the hours with the noose tightening around Eve's neck.

I used my former, smaller body, before adopting the giant one in my battle against Eve's giant one. It stood five feet ten —human height. Covered with plastic, my torso was rather thick, giving me the appearance of a burly man. The legs and arms were easy, though it was a trick to pat the plastic into folds at my joints. I cut my flat feet-plates down, to the proportions of a human foot. Covered with clothes, the imperfections of my pseudo-human body weren't glaring. The important thing was that my hard metal was covered with a softer medium.

Molding my face and hands took the most delicate labor. They would be exposed to constant sight. Jack and Kay were my faithful assistants. Tom was down in the city, delving into the case.

My hands came out as big hams, worthy of a prize-fighter. The fingers were rather stiff, because of the metal "bone" beneath. Jack carefully set human hair into the plastic, over the knuckles, in keeping with my general appearance as a big, brawny man. He molded my facial features with a master's touch—outjutting chin, heavy straight lips, low forehead. He couldn't resist giving me a slight pug nose and a cauliflower ear. Over my shiny skull he glued a wig of matty black hair. And a rather heavy mustache on my upper lip, to conceal the fact that it didn't move when I talked.

The eyes were a problem. I made them myself, two little hemispheres of clear thin glass. My vision was somewhat distorted, and it was a blue world after Jack applied blue-stain for irises.

Kay did her part, rougeing the cheeks and lips cleverly, to take away the dead-flesh texture. Little touches of cosmetics around the eyes and nose blended the features properly.

"There!" Jack grunted finally, with his irrepressible sense of humor. "Didn't know I was a master sculptor down underneath."

They surveyed me critically, from top to toe. I wore a dark tweed suit and a cap pulled low. Suddenly, though they tried to resist, they burst out laughing. I could not blame them when I looked in a full-length mirror.

In the glare of electric light, I was perhaps the strangest looking being imaginable. A big, hulking-shouldered man with a dead "pan" and clumsy arms and legs. Jack stopped laughing and substituted a shaded lamplight for the overhead glare. And there, in the half-gloom with imperfections hidden, I suddenly came to life.

"You'll do," Jack nodded soberly. "You can work only at night, though. And keep out of bright lights. Outside of a certain stiffness in your carriage—which might come from being muscle-bound like any has-been fighter—you're Pete Larch, the pug."

They gave me lessons in walking and swinging my arms naturally. I learned to slouch a little, and take short strides instead of my long, ponderous ones. A rough job, all in all, but we only had two weeks. I would pass for a human to all but the most searching eyes in bright light.

"One thing, though," Jack said worriedly. "That damned jingling noise you make inside." He had the answer to that quickly. He drew out a large watch that made a loud ticking. "Put it in your vest pocket. Kay never liked it anyway. At strategic moments, take it out, so they think it's just that turnip clattering away, and not your gear-and-cog innards. Well, Adam old boy—go out and get your man."

He had tried to lighten the moment I left them with a flippant tone. But beneath it we were solemn. I had a big job ahead of me, with no inkling of how it would come out.

I contacted Eve as I drove toward the city on my errand. The ESP radio-beam oscillator was in my chest-space, connected to my battery for power, with push-button controls wired into my trouser belt.

"Eve! I'm starting out now to find the murderers who hope to see you pay for their crimes. Be patient, loved one."

"I will, Adam. I trust you. I know you'll save me."

I parked the car in a downtown garage, then strode toward the criminal quarter of town. I chose the least frequented streets, where lamplights were dim. Whenever I approached another pedestrian, I watched him narrowly. Most humans unconsciously glance at someone passing. Their glances at me showed nothing of surprise or suspicion. Only at times, a slight repugnance. A wholly naturally reaction, in that I was no debonair fashion-plate, but a seedy, degenerate looking individual.

I was satisfied, as I went along. My human disguise, despite first misgivings, was adequate.

In the criminal quarter, I made my way toward one of the "dives" that were distributed in the neighborhood, frequented by hoodlums, gunmen and all specimens of the lower element. Jack had named three of the places as the most likely hangout for members of the ring we were after. The one victim, Pucelli, pinned the crimes on a certain organization that Jack knew about from his newspaper work.

"Probably the biggest, most powerful gang in the city," Jack had said. "Racketeers, strong-arm men, kidnappers—they've had their hand in everything vicious. The rumor is that the brains, or Boss, of the outfit is a well-protected, solid citizen, known only to his organization. You can't get at him. Just try to find out who did the actual killings, at his orders. Tom will do the rest."

I paused, outside the dive. Adam Link, detective, took a breath—figuratively, at least. Pete Larch walked in.

The dive was noisy, smoke-filled, dim. Thankful for that, I slumped in a chair in a dark corner. A bartender came.

"Whiskey," I ordered, in a low gruff voice, striving to hide its mechanical inflection.

"Chaser?"

"Soda."

Jack had posted me on all these trivial, yet important details. The drink came and I tossed down the coins. The bartender gave me a searching glance. For a moment I was stunned. Did he suspect? Had I done something wrong, in my guise as a human? Then I realized that in a place such as this, every human was given an inspection. A once-over. He shrugged slightly, and from that I gathered that he had put me down as a common drifter.

To anyone observing me, I must have given the impression of a morose chap with nothing to do, here for a few drinks, unconcerned with anyone else. I was quite the contrary. My photo-electric eyes—my real vision behind the glass camouflage —took in every individual in the place. My sensitive tympanums, behind their plastic dummies, were listening to every conversation in the room. To every word whispered between men seated in a far corner, for instance. I have the capacity to select sounds, from behind a background of din.

Sixty feet away, with a tinny piano banging in between, I heard one man mutter to another: "So I says to him, I says, look here—"

Senseless, brainless mouthings. I began to wonder, as I listened all over the room, what life meant to these creatures. It was all so pitifully meaningless. Dr. Link, my creator, did not tell me that so much of humanity drinks the dregs of existence. That so many of his fellow beings were further removed from him, in mentality, than I could ever be.

It happened so quickly, I had no chance to think.

A soft form plumped into my lap. I looked around at one of the painted women whose shrill voices and hard laughter filled the room.

"All alone, big boy?" she said in false sweetness. "Come on,

pep up. Have a little fun. You look like a funeral on two feet."
My plastic face, of course, could not smile.

Her arm slipped about my shoulders, where the plastic-padding was thin. "Mm, hard as nails, aren't you? And you feel cold. You need some warming up—"

Her face came closer, lips puckered. I'm afraid my reaction was rather abrupt. She could not press her lips against my artificial ones! I pushed her off, almost violently.

"Say, you—" Fury blazed from her eyes, as she nearly fell to the floor. "I'll have you know I'm a lady."

"Sorry," I muttered, aware she must be pacified. "I don't feel well. Here, have my drink."

I had been contemplating tossing it on the floor anyway. She downed it in a gulp, smiled, and edged back toward me.

"Get going," I muttered, remembering a man had used that expression before to one of the girls he apparently didn't like.

"Okay, okay—" And she moved off, curling her lip.

The whole episode amused me, as I think it must you too.

CHAPTER 12

The Big Clue

I left the place hours later without the slightest clue of any sort. The other two places Jack had mentioned were similar. I haunted them night after night, desperately. In the daytime, I stayed at Jack's apartment, not willing to risk my disguise against daylight. I began to despair. A precious week had slipped by.

I contacted Eve with radio-telepathy every day, too, but only for a few seconds. The current used up could not be spared too freely. I had a two-week battery within me, and could not replace it except by scraping away my chest-plastic. That would waste time.

Jack and Kay touched me up at times, keeping up my near-human disguise. They had plastic ready, at their place, in case some of mine came off.

One short week left. . . .

And then one night my brain leaped.

I was in one of the pleasure-dives, playing poker with four men. I played for the reason that sitting night after night alone pointed a conspicuous finger at me. Also, I must confess, I had enjoyed the game when playing with Jack and his friends at one time. Periodically I pulled out my loudly-ticking watch, so that they would mistake its noise for my internal sounds. I watched them closely. They never suspected.

The man across eyed my perfect "poker" face uncertainly, shuffling his hand. "You bluffing again?" he suggested. My reaction was a complete blank. "Nope," he finally decided. "Ain't worth five bucks to me. You got my straight beat or you wouldn't have raised me twice." He threw down his cards.

I quietly slipped my king-ten-seven-four-deuce into the deck and raked in the pot. More chips were stacked before me than the others had together.

"You play a mean game, Pete. You sit there like a mummy. You don't even move your eyes. You really concentrate."

I laughed within myself. If they had only known that little more than one-tenth of my brain was on this trivial game. All the while, my full mental powers were concentrated on scanning the room and tuning in methodically from conversation to conversation. I focused on two men hunched over a table, heads together, across the room.

"The orders from the Boss is to lay low, see?" one man murmured. "After that metal dame gets the works, we can go to town again."

Senseless talk, like all the rest.

"Cut?" The game again, demanding one-tenth of my attention.

I cut with my big hand. I was about to eavesdrop elsewhere, in the meantime, when it leaped out at me—*metal dame*. I had caught on to some of the twisted slang in use, in the past week.

Metal dame meant Eve.

It was my first lead.

I didn't move. I didn't give the slightest sign that I was straining to hear more. The two men were fifty feet away. Between was a confused babble and clinking of glasses. It was all my sharp, selective tympanums could do to separate their whispers from the extraneous noise.

"Who's on the job?" asked the other man.

"You in, Pete?"—the card game again—"How many cards?"

I tossed in a chip and threw one card away. I had four sevens.

Names were mentioned, in a guarded whisper fifty feet away, that no human ear could have heard from five feet. "They're meeting at the warehouse, near Larkin's, tomorrow night. But we don't go, the Boss says. We—"

"Two to stay in, Pete. You raise two? Raise you two. You're bluffing, this time. You drew one to a full-house, but I've got aces up. Two to you."

"—lay low. Let the metal dame burn for you and me, first."

"Okay. I'm going; get some shut-eye."

"Me, too."

"What you got, Pete? Fours! Damn it, you ain't human."

Instead of gathering in the pot, I shoved all my winnings away. "Divide it up, boys," I said rising. My eye was on the two men weaving their way to the door. The two murderers in whose place Eve was to be sentenced to the electric chair.

I moved too fast, however, in my eagerness. I bumped against a heavy-set man just passing our table. He staggered back, then straightened, glaring at me.

"Watch who you're bumping, you clumsy bum," he roared. "I'll teach you—"

"It's Slug O'Leary," gasped a voice. "He'll kill the poor guy—" Meaning me.

He came at me with swinging arms, obviously short-tempered. He was a giant of a man, solidly built, with arms thick

91

as posts. His fist came straight for my head. He met nothing. I had dodged, with a swiftness given me by reflexes triggered with speedy electrons. Recovering his balance, bellowing in rage, he swung three more times in split-seconds. Unfulfilled blows that would have knocked any human out. Or would have broken his arm if they had touched me. My head weaved aside, easily avoiding the haymakers.

The semi-circle of watchers who had quickly bunched around us stared in disbelief. They had never seen anyone dodge that fast. Humiliated, Slug O'Leary came at me with new tactics, extending his great arms for a bear-hug. He tugged, expecting to lift me off the floor and fling me down bodily. I wonder what he thought as my 500 pounds remained glued to the floor.

He tugged again, mightily, his face red with strain and fury. I felt a little of my plastic, in back, give way. To break his hold before further damage, I hugged him in turn. I squeezed slightly. His breath went out in a gust. One of his ribs cracked a little. I let loose then and he staggered back, amazed.

Amazed, but not beaten. I was forced to admire his courage as he caught his breath, growled like a wounded bear, and plunged again. I could not risk another encounter. He might tear away part of my disguise. I had to get rid of him and follow my quarry.

I would have to hit him, although I had never, in my two years of life, struck a person before. It had been my steadfast resolve never to use brute power to gain my ends, and thus label the intelligent robot as a monster to be feared.

But now I had to, for the sake of Eve.

My arm came out. I pulled the punch as much as I could, knowing too well of the levered power behind it. It landed squarely on his chin, with a sharp crack. Slug O'Leary's knees bent and he slumped to the floor without a sound.

"Knocked cold," said an awed voice from the crowd. "First time I saw Slug get it."

I stared down at the fallen man. Within me for a moment I was—well sick. I had struck a human being. I wonder if you humans consider that as utterly repulsive and degrading as I did, using the methods of the beast.

The ring of watchers cheered. Hero of the moment, they crowded around me, slapping my back. Stinging their hands, undoubtedly, and marveling at my hard "muscle". I groaned within. I almost bellowed for them to get out of my way. I wanted nothing of their stupid acclaim. I wanted only to get out, after the two men. They were gone already. But I couldn't get through that press of crowd without using rough methods.

92

My plastic wouldn't stand rough handling. And another display of my strength would brand me for what I was.

Something warned me not to risk it. Adam Link, detective, must not yet be exposed. I allowed my card-playing friends to hustle me to the bar, and a drink was placed before me.

"I really have to go—" I mumbled.

"Aw, you've got time for one drink at least," one insisted. "Pete, old boy, you're a grand guy. Look, he ain't even breathing heavy. Grand guy—"

I basked in that for a moment. Somehow, it felt good to be treated like a human, even by these rough-cut creatures. Perhaps my first judgment of their kind was too harsh.

"Come on, drink up." Glasses were raised—to me.

It was the only way. I tossed the liquid between my plastic lips. I felt it trickle past my metal larynx. Stupidly, I had not foreseen such a circumstance. And now I felt the liquid begin to drop down upon exposed wires.

Hastily I mumbled excuses and turned away. By their conventions, I was now free to go. Slug O'Leary came toward me near the door. They had dashed water in his face, bringing him around, apparently none the worse for the blow. I tensed. Would I never get out?

He stuck out his hand, grinning. "Pal, you're the first man has licked me in five years. Shake."

Outside the place at last, I felt a peculiar glow within me. But not only from that gesture. The drink had now trickled down on wires, creating a short. As I stepped down the street, I was weaving. It is amusing, even to me, to think that one drink has far more "kick" for me than for any human. The short had upset my electrical spirit-level system that keeps my balance.

"Drunk as a Lord," commented a man to his companion as they passed.

It was a new sensation to me, vaguely pleasurable. But sharp warning clicked in my brain. I hurried. I went down alleys wherever I could, breaking into a staggering run. I reached Jack's apartment and collapsed on his doorstep.

"Quick!" I was barely able to mutter. "Disconnect me for an hour—"

When they reconnected me, the liquid had evaporated and I was myself. I told my story.

"Those were the two 'trigger' men, then," Jack said. "Though they varied it with metal clubs that night, to involve Eve. You didn't get their names? You'll have to go back and wait for them to show up again."

I pondered. "If I do, and trail them, will it lead to the man who gave them orders?" I asked.

"The Big Boss?" Jack shook his head. "No. He told them to lay low—which means to keep away from him. The best we can do is identify the two killers and let Tom fight it out in court."

"I'll prove in court," said Tom "that the metal filings weren't from Eve's body. Then I'll indict the two killers."

"But in the meantime," I said slowly, "The man really responsible—the Big Boss—goes free?"

Jack pounded his fist into his other palm. "I just wish we could get him. He's the mainspring of the most vicious, powerful crime ring in this city. But it's out of the question—"

"Is it?" My thoughts were clashing, grinding. The actual killers caught; Eve freed, perhaps—but the brain who had played with them all as pawns would be untouched, unpunished.

"Where is that warehouse, near Larkin's?" I said. "I'm going there tomorrow night."

"Don't be a fool," Jack retorted. "Waste of precious time. No one can uncover that ring in one short week."

"Not even Adam Link, detective?" I said.

The next night, following Jack's instructions, I headed for the warehouse district, near the criminal quarter. There was a dive called "Larkin's Pleasure Palace". Back of it, as Jack had said, loomed a huge dark warehouse. In there, four men were meeting, part of the Big Boss's crime ring. I could not find a way in from the street level. I saw the first level of a fire-escape, ladder pulled up. Flexing my legs, I leaped straight up ten feet, catching a metal bar and swinging myself onto the first landing. I made no noise. I weigh 500 pounds, but I have more timing and absolute control over motion than any circus acrobat. I say these things without false modesty. They are facts.

I clambered up the fire escape quietly, and found an open skylight on the roof. From there I took a running broad-jump of some thirty feet to a flat metal beam running across the warehouse's interior. Here I perched silently, listening.

I heard the low murmur of voices a hundred feet away, from behind boxes stacked to the roof. I dropped to the floor into a pile of excelsior. It deadened my landing to a low thud. I crouched, listening, but they hadn't heard. I made my way—tiptoed, you might say—to a position behind the rampart of boxes. From behind I could distinguish their words clearly.

They seemed to be plotting some nefarious business, but in language whose criminal idiom escaped me. It was something about a kidnapping. I was not concerned with that. Only with something relating to the Big Boss—or Eve. I began to wonder if my quest would be useless.

94

Then I tensed.

"Okay," that's settled," one man's voice said. He laughed. "The Boss says that way we'll pin it on the robot again—on the other one, Adam Link. What a couple of tin monkeys he's making out of them. Joe and Lefty are laying low till the metal skirt takes the rap for them. Boy, the Boss sure has brains."

"Yeah," agreed another. "And pretty soon he'll be on the City Tax Council, cutting us in on easy graft and big money. That'll be sweet—Councillor Harvey Brigg—"

"Shut your trap," hissed the first man. "Hasn't the Boss warned us never to mention his name?"

"Aw, who's going to hear—"

Again he was interrupted. "Which one of you guys is sportin' that loud ticker?"

There was silence for a moment.

I should have been warned. But I hardly heard. Only one thing drummed in my mind—Harvey Brigg. I knew his name. The name of the man who had plotted three murders in the name of my innocent Eve.

Suddenly two ugly automatics were pointing at me, from both sides at once. The men had come around the boxes. I could have leaped away, easily, even then. But again something warned me not to risk exposure of my identity. Better to act the part of a human, caught like a rat in a trap.

They prodded me around the boxes to where they had sat. A flickering candle lighted the scene. They peered at me in its dim rays. The illusion of my human disguise held, fortunately.

"A dick, eh?" barked the leader of the four. "The Boss warned us to watch for dicks working for Adam Link. How much did you hear?"

I maintained a silence.

"We'll make you talk, smart guy. Barney, find some rope."

They tied me flat against a box, standing upright. Then, after ripping my chest free of the coat and shirt, they held burning matches to my "flesh". I acted the part of a man in torment, with what histrionic ability I could summon. I squirmed against my bonds and made low moans. But I held my squirmings in check, lest the cords break.

I only hoped they wouldn't penetrate my disguise. Luckily, the stench of the plastic under the flame was not much different from seared human flesh. I gathered that from their rather sickened expressions. I have no sense of smell.

"Guess he won't talk," said one of the men. They had burned welts all over my plastic chest. They could not hide a certain grudging admiration, thinking me a human with remarkable fortitude.

One of the men fidgeted. "Maybe he heard everything—even the Boss's name."

They looked at each other. The light that gleamed in their eyes made even me shudder. It is the look of human beings about to kill another.

"Okay, wise guy," snapped the leader. "You won't talk dead any more than alive. Let him have it, boys."

Their guns spoke in chorus. The heavy slugs thudded into my chest plastic, in a barrage. Carrying my part of the last, I slumped back against the box, head lolling. One of the men grabbed my wrist and felt for the pulse.

"No heart-beat," he announced. "Dead."

Calmly the leader then flipped the lighted candle to the floor, kicking a pile of excelsior toward it.

"They won't even find the body," he exulted. "Come on, boys—"

They left my "dead" body. They had done the job too quickly to notice three things: that there was no blood on my chest, that my eyes hadn't closed, and under the roar of guns they hadn't heard the bullets making a muffled ring, as they struck against metal under the plastic.

I waited five minutes, just to be sure. They were gone. Then I straightened, up, and walked away from the box, hardly aware of the heavy rope snapping like string around me. A ring of fire licked about me. I walked through it, not feeling the flame that burned half my clothes off before I noticed and beat it out with my hands. I climbed to the skylight, went down the fire-escape, and through an alley. At the corner I pulled the fire-alarm I found there. No need to let valuable property burn down.

I made my way down dark streets to Jack's place. Within I was laughing, laughing. I wondered what those four gangsters would think if they could see the "man" they had "bumped off" walking along with his "riddled" body. But then I sobered. Adam Link, detective, faced his biggest assignment of all—tracking down the master criminal Harvey Brigg.

CHAPTER 13

Robot Rescue

I called Eve on the radio-telepathy. Poor Eve, sitting there in her cell twenty-four hours a day, waiting, hoping, perhaps despairing.

"Adam, I want to come to you," she said almost immediately. "I cannot stand these horrible walls, and the chains binding me, and the cold stares of the prison people. Adam, let me come—"

Don't forget that Eve—mentally—was a young, sensitive girl. Not a cold, passionless being of steel nerves. Think of your sister or wife in jail.

"Eve, dear," I said gently, firmly. "You must trust me. It is only a few days now. And then you will be free. I swear it."

Kay, at Jack's apartment, gave a little shriek as I walked in. Small wonder. My clothes were tatters, half burned away, exposing plastic that was seared and blackened. My "chest" was a ruin of what looked like torn dead flesh, with metal shining through in places. The metal was dented where the slugs had struck. My nose was gone. Somewhere it had been knocked off. I remembered now the rather shocked glances of the few pedestrians I had passed in the late hour. But they had shrugged and walked on, perhaps disbelieving most of what they saw so dimly.

Jack laughed too, when I told the story. "You took *them* for a ride." Then he sobered, grinding his teeth. "Harvey Brigg, of all people. Unimpeachable character—in daily life. Lives in a swell home in a respectable neighborhood. But Adam, we're stumped now. You couldn't get anything on him in a year's trying, much less a few days."

"I'll wring a confession out of him," I returned harshly. My hands were working.

"Adam!" It was Kay's voice. She was peering at me in a shocked way.

I understood immediately. In her eyes—the disguise aside —I was a man, a human—a big strong man, but gentle in nature. It was not like me to speak of brutal methods, no matter what the circumstances.

"Sorry, Kay. Don't fear that I've changed. It's just that my blood boils, like that of any decent man's, thinking of

97

Harvey Brigg." I spent a few seconds thinking. "A dictaphone. Jack, get me a dictaphone."

"Wire it into his house?" Jack snorted. "My God, man, do you think you're a wizard?"

"Wires? I won't need wires. Get me the dictaphone and then drive me to my mountain laboratory."

In the laboratory, I worked all the next day over the dictaphone Jack procured. It was simple, in a way, to eliminate the need of wires. In some basic mechanical principles, you human technicians are backward. Many things lie just before your nose. My creator Dr. Link—I mean no irreverence— spent years devising my body. In six months after I had come to life, I had improved my body four-fold.

Jack and Kay also patched up my torn chest with new plastic, remodeled a nose, and touched up my disguise in general. A new suit of clothes replaced the rags.

The next night I was behind the hedges of Harvey Brigg's large home, with a black satchel. After some study, I climbed the roof of a back porch, careful so that I came up with barely a slither of my shoes. I forced the lock of an attic window. By leaning my weight slowly and steadily in the strategic spot, the latch clinked apart like nothing more than a snapping stick.

Inside, I wound my way past dust-covered old furniture and trunks. Wherever a board under my feet threatened to creak, I let my weight down with measured slowness, changing the sharp sound to a soft rubbing of wood. At certain places I kneeled, with my head touching the floor. Sounds from below, conducted through the walls, vibrated into my mechanical tympanums. The attic, to human ears, would have been as silent as a tomb, I suppose.

I will not detail the hours I snooped in this way, gradually learning, by sound alone, what rooms were below and who was in them. Three servants had retired. A fourth stood in a hall and later let in a late caller. He was led to a room that I knew to be Harvey Brigg's private office or den.

The door closed, down below. The two men were alone. "Well, Shane?" asked a cultured voice. "How did the job go?"

I hated the voice the moment I heard it. The voice of Harvey Brigg. Oily, smug, with hard overtones. The voice of a man whose heart was harder than the metal parts of my distributor "heart".

Quickly, I rigged up my dictaphone system. I laid its pickup device for sound on the floor. Like my ears, it was sensitive to the faint vibrations working through. If needed I could have made it sensitive to the chirping of a cricket in the basement.

I had already connected the battery from my satchel. I tripped the on-stud. Five miles away, in Jack's apartment, I knew the tape-recorder was taking down what the pick-up mike sent out as electronic impulses. At the same time, I leaned down on the floor, listening for myself.

"It went okay, Boss," the visitor, Shane, said. "But a gumshoe dick was on the trail. Horned in on the boys at the warehouse. They couldn't make him talk so they plugged him, and set fire to the joint. Morning paper told how the fire was put out after burning half the stuff in there. But nobody was mentioned so the body must have burned to ashes. Good work, eh, Boss?"

I could picture them grinning at one another triumphantly. But I was grinning—in my mind—more than they, and for better reason.

"Wonder if that Adam Link put him on the job?" mused Harvey Brigg's voice. "Adam Link is supposed to be a mental wizard, robot or not—" There was just a shade of apprehension in his tone.

"But he don't compare with you, Boss," Shane responded. "You've got twice the brains he has."

"I think you're right, Shane," Harvey Brigg agreed readily. "Four days from now his partner robot goes to trial. A little planning to pin it on the robot, and three men I had on the Black List were rubbed out. And who gets blamed? Who will take the rap? Not Joe and Lefty."

There was loud laughter for a moment. Then Brigg's voice came again. "Eve Link, the Frankenstein robot, takes the rap. Read that book sometime, Shane. You'll know why then, at the trial, the jury will slap a guilty verdict on the robot faster than greased lightning. Evidence pro or con won't matter. It'll be just that they'll be *ready* to believe the robot did it. I had that all figured out, you see."

I had listened with riveted attention. Two things were clear: Harvey Brigg was a megalomaniac and second, he was dead right about the trial—or had been. I don't know which burned in me stronger at that moment. Anger at his cold, deadly plan in involving Eve. Or singing triumph that his own voice on tape would betray him.

The master-mind who had twice the brains of Adam Link spoke again. "Shane, you're a smart boy yourself. But now about the kidnapping. Give me all the details."

Shane went into a recital of the kidnapping. It had been an efficient, cold-blooded job, taking a young woman away from her well-to-do husband. Then their discussion went into

99

other channels—store robbery, protection fees, even the sale of drugs. Shane, I gathered as I listened, was the sole go-between for Brigg and his widespread "gang". Brigg outlined certain methods of procedure, with a calm efficiency.

As the minutes slipped by, I was amazed at the ramifications of his ring. I began to doubt he could be a human being. He must be a frightful monster, human in name only.

The visitor left after two hours. I heard Brigg get into bed. I sat thinking. My mission was over. Eve was safe. But I thought of more than Eve. I thought of a city of humans preyed upon by this spider and his minions.

There were four days left before the trial. I stayed for three in the attic of Harvey Brigg's home. I did not need food or water. I did not get cramped muscles, sitting for long hours. I signaled Eve once and told her to tell Kay of my decision to stay, so they wouldn't worry about me.

No one disturbed me—except once. A servant was suddenly climbing the attic stairs. I had no chance to run for any item of furniture large enough to hide me. I was exposed to plain view, twenty feet from the stairwell. What could I do? I sat utterly still.

It was a woman. She came up and glanced around, looking for something. Her face turned my way. I froze into complete immobility. Her eyes flicked past me, safely.

I can offer a non-miraculous explanation. The light was dim. My absolute stillness must have deceived her into taking me for an inanimate object—perhaps a bundle of rags. No human being could have escaped. For no human can duplicate the rigidity of something non-living and non-breathing, as I can.

As for not hearing me—my internal hum and jingling seemed loud in the confined attic—I knew she was hard of hearing. Brigg had revealed once, in the course of his conversations, that he picked his servants for their poor hearing, thus safeguarding himself from any eavesdropping by them.

She went to a trunk, rummaged within, and left. I began to breathe again—no, sometimes I forget I am not human. I felt relieved, however.

No other disturbance came, and I went on with my recording. During the day, Brigg was out much of the time. But often he was in, and would closet himself with Shane, discussing their sinister activities in business-like tones. All of this poured into the super-ear of my instrument, and from that device invisibly to the tape-recorder in Jack's apartment. I had enough, in three days, to damn Brigg in the eyes of any court.

On the third night, something significant came from below.

Shane was there again. It was near midnight. They were discussing the kidnapping.

"But he claims, Boss," Shane was saying, "that he can't raise more than $40,000 by midnight. He wants more time."

Harvey Brigg's voice was adamant. "Fifty thousand dollars by midnight was our stipulation. Since he can't, or won't pay, his wife dies at midnight. Go to the shack now, Shane. At midnight sharp—unless our contact man comes with the money—tell the boys to bash in her skull with the metal bar."

I could sense that even Shane shuddered at Brigg's utterly merciless tone. "But hell, Boss—"

"That's an order, you fool. Don't you understand? This kidnapping doesn't count so much. The killing will be pinned on Adam Link, the robot. When we pull other kidnappings, they'll pay up promptly, thinking it's the cold-blooded, ruthless robot from whom they can expect no mercy."

And not knowing—the thought drummed in my brain—that it was the cold-blooded, ruthless Harvey Brigg from whom they could expect no mercy.

"I get it, Boss. It'll make the other kidnappings a cinch."

"Get going," snapped Brigg. "At midnight, remember."

At midnight, a woman was to die. I was the only one who knew of it. I couldn't let it happen particularly since I would be blamed. I left the attic, where I had been for three days and nights. I moved as swiftly and quietly as I could, leaped from the porch to soft grass, and scurried behind a hedge. Shane's car backed out of the drive and roared away with a clash of gears.

I followed, with an equal clash of gears. For the first time in my two weeks of sleuthing, I let out my full running powers. I passed one late pedestrian. The man stopped stock-still, whirled to watch me, and then staggered to the curb and sat down, apparently sick. I saw that briefly over my shoulder. I might have been amused, except that my mission was so grim.

I pounded after Shane's car as it left the outskirts of the town where Brigg lived. Traffic was sparse as he passed into the countryside. Shane hit up a good speed. I ran along the concrete road's shoulder, about a block behind Shane's car, so that he wouldn't glimpse me in his rear-vision mirror. Auto headlights momentarily lit me up—a human figure racing at better than 70 miles an hour. I don't think the oncoming cars realized my speed. But the two or three I passed, going my way, must have. I can only surmise, as you can, what the drivers thought as what seemed a man over-hauled and shot past them, though their motors were roaring.

I felt a certain exhilaration, using my full machine powers, after the days in the attic. I suppose it is something like a

101

confined man feeling glad when he gets out and uses his muscles for a change. I raced along after the tail-light of Shane's car, my internal mechanisms humming smoothly. Yet I am glad the pace did not keep up long. I hadn't oiled and checked myself over for two weeks.

Twenty minutes later Shane's car slowed and turned down a rutty road that presently wound into an isolated woods. Finally it went down what was little more than a weed-grown trail, barely wide enough for the car. It stopped near an old shack, before which another car was parked. I crouched behind the trunk of a tree.

Figures came out with guns in hand, greeted Shane, and they went in. It was one minute to midnight. I did not look at my watch to tell that. I have a sense of absolute time. I know what time it is at any second of the day or night.

In one minute, a woman was to die.

I crept to the shack door, placing my head against the wood to hear. I heard their voices.

"No word from Slick, our contact man?" Shane queried.

"Nope. The $50,000 didn't come. What's the boss's orders, Shane?"

He must have made a silent signal, perhaps with a little spark of pity for the woman who must be awake and listening. I heard the men grunt a little, and one muttered, "Half a minute to midnight."

"Where's my husband?" sounded a feminine voice, strained and half-hysterical. "You told me he'd be coming soon—"

That was all I had been waiting for—the sound of her voice. Rather, its position. She was in the rear of the one-room shack. She should be safe from what would happen.

Now was the moment.

Within me, my distributor clicked over little automatic relays that released a flood of electricity through my steely frame. With one blow of my fist I splintered the door in half. I sprang into the room.

Five startled men jerked around. One was in the corner, just picking up a metal angle-iron, ready to crash it down on the skull of the young woman lying bound on a rickety couch. Four pairs of eyes popped, for, with the exception of Shane, they had all seen me before. They were the four who had met at the warehouse.

"God Almighty!" gasped one. "It's the dick we pumped full of lead—"

Their guns barked immediately. I walked straight into the hail of lead. I strode for the man with the bar, jerked it out of his hands, bent it into a loop. Somehow, I had to do that

102

first. It was the instrument of murder which was to have pinned the deed on me.

Then I grabbed the man's gun. He had just fired pointblank at my chest. I crushed it in my hand and flung the pieces at the others. I went for them, but they had stopped firing. They stood like frozen images, faces dead white. The fear in their hearts shone from their blood shot eyes. *Who was this man who could not be killed?*

I stood in the center of the room, defying them.

Shane deliberately raised his gun and aimed for my head. I dodged the bullet, moving my head a split-second before his finger squeezed the trigger. A shot in my eyes would do damage. Shane shot again at my head. Again it thudded into the wall beyond. It was like an act in a strange drama. Shane shot at my chest, still with that slow, paralyzed incredulity. The slug spanked with a metallic clang. A dawning look came into his face.

"Cripes," he whispered. "It's Adam Link."

With shrieks, they scrambled for the door, clawing at each other to get out. I let them get into their car, outside, then grasped the bumper and overturned it. They piled into Shane's car and I overturned that, spilling them out. They ran for the woods.

CHAPTER 14

Human Monster

I let them go. I had no wish to harm them. Poor misguided wretches, they were only pawns in the horrible game played by Harvey Brigg. He was the man my slow anger was directed against.

I went into the shack. The woman, who had fainted during the battle, was just opening her eyes. She did not seem any too reassured now, though I had routed her abductors.

"Who are you" she quavered.

"A detective," I said. If I had said Adam Link, her already strained, haggard mind might have snapped completely. As it was, when I snapped her cords apart like flimsy cotton and picked her up with the ease of a little doll, she gasped. I carried her to Shane's car, retrieved it from the ditch, and drove off.

"Where do you live?" I asked, as I turned on the highway.

She gave me the address. "You'll be home safe in nineteen minutes," I told her.

She smiled then. Perhaps her feminine intuition told her I was a friend. A moment later I saw her head back against the cushion. She was sleeping as peacefully as a baby. Good thing, perhaps. I drove that nineteen-minute stretch to town at a wild pace that would have thrown her into hysteria again. Wild? My driving, at ninety an hour, is safer than that of any human at twenty.

She was able to walk up the steps of her home, holding my arm. She fell into the arms of her husband, both choking in joy. I left. I wasn't needed any more. In Shane's car, I drove toward Jack's apartment.

Everything had turned out splendidly. I congratulated myself. Tomorrow was Eve's trial. In Jack's apartment was the evidence that would free Eve and convict Harvey Brigg. His treacherous ring would be broken.

I called Eve on the radio-telepathy, telling her the wonderful news. I had not wanted to make any false promises till now, when I was sure of myself. She interrupted me, excitedly.

"Adam! Why haven't you contacted me sooner? Jack and

104

Tom have been hoping to get in touch with you, through me. Tom was just in my cell this evening again—"

"What's wrong?" I snapped. "Didn't the recording come through?" It was the only thing I could think of. Yet it couldn't be that. I had made thorough tests before taking the apparatus to Brigg's home. But fool, I told myself, why couldn't I at least have checked with Jack? At times, you see, I have quite human failings and lack of reasoning.

"Yes, most of it," Eve returned. "But the first part, three days ago, came through with lots of static. Tom says the voices are so distorted that it won't hold in court."

"The first part?" I went a little cold. "That was the part where Brigg revealed his three murders pinned on you. Eve, what else did Tom say?"

"Tom is worried. He says that although he has enough to indict Brigg on almost everything else, he won't be able to clear me in time. Brigg will fight his case with powerful lawyers. In the meantime, my trial will have to go on and—well, Tom won't say any more."

I was stunned. I knew what it meant. Eve tried, convicted, and executed long before Harvey Brigg's legal defenses could be battered down. Without that vital bit of dictaphone evidence, destroyed by static, I had gotten nowhere.

Her telepathy-voice came again. "Adam, I'm so lonesome for you. I want to come to you. There is no hope now anyway—"

"Eve, no!" My thoughts crackled. "Eve, you must stay there. Don't despair, darling. There is still a way—"

I clicked off. I wrenched the car around in the street on two wheels for a U-turn. I arrived at Brigg's home in a few minutes. I strode up the front steps to the door, rang the bell boldly.

The servant who opened the door said, "Come in, Shane." I had arrived in Shane's car. But in the hall light, he started. "You're not Shane. Who are you? What do you want?"

"I want to see Harvey Brigg," I said.

"You can't—"

I pushed him aside as though he were a rag dummy and strode for the room I knew to be Brigg's den—or lair. I yanked open the door, walked in.

Brigg looked up from a desk. I was as startled as he. I had expected to see a depraved looking man. Instead he was tall, upright, with smiling features and straightforward blue eyes. No one would suspect him for a master criminal—as no one had.

He frowned. "Haven't I told you men you must never come to see me personally? Only Shane is allowed—"

"I'm not one of your men, Harvey Brigg," I interposed. "I'm your enemy. I know you for the utter scoundrel you are. You gave the orders that murdered Deering, Pucelli and Unger. Write out and sign a confession to that effect immediately, absolving Eve Link."

Brigg's blue eyes had narrowed.

"So Adam Link's detectives figured it all out? But how foolish to come here for my confession. You don't think I can be intimidated like a schoolboy?" An amused smile hovered over his full lips.

"You will sign that confession or—" My dry mechanical tones hid the deadly hiss in my meaning. I took a step forward.

"It would interest you to know that my servant—or bodyguard—has you covered." Brigg nonchalantly waved in back of me.

I looked. The servant-bodyguard I had swept past was calmly leaning in the doorway with a gun pointing at me.

Just as calmly, I spoke. "At your shack, a half-hour ago, your kidnappers emptied their guns at me. If you look close, you can see the holes in my suit."

I held out my palms, where the plastic had been worn off, exposing the telescoping joints of my metal fingers. I also deliberately clawed at the plastic of my face. The seeming flesh came away in rubbery shreds. There was no blood. The false face fell away to reveal my true one of featureless metal.

"I am Adam Link," I said simply.

The two men recoiled as if an atomic bomb faced them. Then the bodyguard's gun hissed, with a silencer on it. Five slugs made five new holes in my suit. The sixth, aimed at my head, thudded into the wall beyond, as I dodged. The thug stared for a moment longer, then bolted with a womanlike shriek from a cowardly soul.

I banged the door shut and faced Harvey Brigg. He was trembling like a leaf.

I spoke at some length.

"Your career is over, Harvey Brigg. I have a dictaphone record of all you and Shane have said in the past three days. But to save Eve Link, my metal mate, I want your written confession for the three murders. The three murders for which, all through the city, they are yelling, 'Frankenstein' at her."

I glared at him. My flat phonic voice showed nothing of the emotion I felt as I went on.

"Eve a Frankenstein monster? You, Harvey Brigg, are the Frankenstein monster, created out of the rottenest of human thoughts and aims. And it is you who wear a mask, not I. I have more right to cover myself with human-looking camouflage than you have to hide behind your screen of uprightness. You, Harvey Brigg, are more of a monster than I or my Eve could ever be."

I leaned over his desk. I placed paper and a pen before him. "Write," I commanded. "Write the words I dictate. 'I, Harvey Brigg, confess to planning and ordering the murders of—'"

He made no move to comply, just sat there staring at me with staggered shock in his face. He grabbed for the telephone suddenly. I snatched it away, ripped out the wire. I reached over, grabbing his left wrist. "I am strong," I said. "I am a machine. I have never before taken the life of a human. I am prepared to tonight, if only to rid the world of you."

The wrist made a little snapping sound suddenly. I had not meant to do it. I had forgotten my powers.

Harvey Brigg made a gasping shriek of pain. He was mortally frightened now.

"Don't!" he groaned. "Don't kill me. I'll write—"

He snatched up the pen with his right hand and began scratching away, fearful that I would tear him to little bits. His fear was not unfounded.

I heard the noise, but took no account of it. I was too wrapped up in watching the words spill down on paper that would free Eve the next day at the trial.

The door burst open. In it were framed the bodyguard, Shane, and the four kidnappers. The latter, obviously, had flagged or forced a car to stop, come back to town, and met the bodyguard outside with his story.

"Get out," I roared, advancing on them and waving my arms. "You know your bullets are useless against me. Get out, you fools."

But they weren't fools. I had underestimated them. I didn't notice till too late what one held in his hand—a bomb-grenade. He pulled the pin and tossed it at my feet. It exploded with a dull thunder.

I swayed, then toppled. The bomb had wrecked my legs. I crashed to the floor. My brain was stunned by the terrific concussion working through my metal body. Another bomb-grenade was raised to finish me off.

"Wait!" It was the voice of Harvey Brigg. He came up out of the splintered wreck of his desk, where he had dived. "Don't throw it. He can't move or run now. Wreck his arms with an axe, while he's still stunned. Hurry. But I want him alive—his brain—for a while."

The bodyguard returned with a fire-axe from the hall and hacked away at my arm-joints. I was still brain-numb, with no command over my mechanisms. The arms were severed soon, gears and muscle cables jangling loose. I was completely helpless, then, like an armless and legless man.

They stood over me, panting. Harvey Brigg looked down at me. His formerly mild, guileless face was twisted in a leer of hate and triumph, as he nursed his broken wrist. He had given another order to his bodyguard. He reappeared with a blow-torch.

"I can't break your wrist and make you suffer," Brigg said to me. "But we'll try this——"

At his order, the blow-torch's hissing flame was applied to my head-piece. All around evenly. The metal began to heat up.

"We'll fry your clever metal brain in its case," gloated the human monster named Harvey Brigg.

Pain came to me, or its equivalent in my robot sensations. The heat began to throw my delicate electron-currents off, creating static that hammered like a frightful headache. I groaned, but this time in reality, not like when matches had been applied to my chest plastic. Diabolically, Harvey Brigg had known this would be torture to me.

Through the pain I heard his voice.

"With you out of the way, Adam Link, your Eve Link goes to the chair for those murders. As for the tape recording your helpers have, I'll fight it tooth and nail. Dictaphone evidence is never conclusive. I have a good chance of going scot-free, or maybe getting convicted on some minor count that won't break up my ring." He laughed derisively. "Adam Link, detective. This is your first and last case. Goodbye!"

I was going fast and he knew it. I felt a little surge of consolation as the man with the blow-torch, kneeling at my side, accidentally hooked his coat in the belt stud of my radio-telepathy unit, turning it on. It was still intact, within my chest space. They knew nothing of the silent telepathic call I sent to Eve.

"Goodbye, my Eve," I called. I gave brief details. "Go through with the trial, as I did once. If you're saved by a miracle, carry on what I have tried to do—show humans that intelligent robots have a place in human society. Goodbye, dearest."

There was nothing more to say. I didn't want to say that there was no hope, not even for a miracle. She would join me in non-existence soon. The advent of robot-life in the world would end with the epitaph—"Died in infancy."

"Adam—"

That was the only word Eve said in return. Or shrieked. It registered as that in my electronic thought currents. When I tried to contact her again, I failed. Some wire or connection had slipped, probably loosened by the bomb concussion before.

That would be my last word from her, I reflected through my agony. "Adam—" It had held a world of meaning. Anguish, loyalty, love. A love, though unbiologic, that equals the highest of your human loves. And in that I felt a calm peace. The peace before death.

In ten minutes my head-case had begun to glow dull red. The outer iridium-sponge cells of my brain were shriveling, melting, paper-thin as they were. I longed for death. But my consciousness clung to my life-current. I was amazed myself at the tenacity of "life" within me. The heat that would have burned a human brain away in seconds had still not conquered mine.

But it would. My thoughts began to reel, plunging down into the pit of extinction. I was half-insane, so far gone that I suddenly imagined I saw Eve's gigantic form standing in the doorway.

"Adam!" the image seemed to cry. "What are they doing to you? Are you still alive—"

Cold shock swept over me, as the blow-torch tumbled from cruel hands and all the men whirled as if shot.

Eve was really there.

Broken lengths of chain still hung from her wrists, ankles and neck. Chain that she had snapped like rotten cord, in one furious tug, after I contacted her. I could surmise the rest. She had wrenched the cell-door off its hinges, brushed screaming jail officials aside, and run out of the prison. She had come in ten minutes across town. She must have run at express-train speed. She must have sent more than one late pedestrian or motorist shrieking for cover, as her giant metal form careened through the night streets. She knew the address, through Tom. She had found the way by sheer instinct, or perhaps by clutching some luckless human in her mighty hands and demanding directions.

All that aside, she was here.

The men were frozen, eyes horrified. Harvey Brigg backed away to a wall and flattened himself against it as though to push through. For they all saw that the creature before them was berserk.

Slowly and steadily she advanced on the seven men cowering in the corner. She thought I was dead, seeing me in a tangled ruin. She was fully intent on crushing those seven men to pulp.

I tried to call out, stop her. But my mechanical larynx was heat-warped to uselessness. I could not make the slightest move, to show I was alive. I could not even click my eye-shutters, to blank out the sight. I would see seven men ground to bloody shreds. More than that, I would see the robot once and for all banished from life in human society, for that act.

"Eve!" I tried to plead. "Eve, don't betray me now. Don't do just what I've warned against from the start. Don't prove the robot is just what the world is too ready to believe—a Frankenstein monster. Eve—please—don't!"

But I couldn't make a sound. My mental agony at the moment was far greater than the heat-torture had been.

Eve was within reach of the men. They were clawing at one another to get out of the way. They too were silent, with fear strangling them. Eve's merciless hands stretched out, for the first victim—

A siren wailed, somewhere outside, moaning to high crescendo. Eve had caught one man, trying to slip past her, and hurled him back in the group, as though intent on making them suffer the suspense of death as well as death itself. She seemed to tense herself for sudden activity, her internal hum deepening. She was about to commit wholesale massacre. . . .

Then blue-clad men were swarming into the room—police. I shrieked and cursed, within myself. She would rend them apart too. She whirled on the police. . . .

At that moment I found my voice. My heated metal had cooled enough for parts to slip into place. It was only a croak, my voice.

"Eve, stop! Submit to the police. Don't touch the men."

She stood in the center of the room, looking from the police to the men, and then down at me—or what was left of me. She made no move against any of them.

The gangsters found their voices. Babbling, they begged the police to protect them from the metal monster.

"Make them confess," I yelled out, my voice stronger now. "Make Harvey Brigg confess to the murders Eve is accused of, and all his other criminal activities."

Eve looked around and fixed her baleful eye-lenses on Harvey Brigg.

"I'll confess," he cried eagerly, frantically. "I'll confess everything. Only don't let that robot touch me."

I have only one more thing to record. We were in our mountain cabin, with Jack, Kay and Tom, court procedure over. I had a new body, and Eve was in her first one, human proportioned.

"We won all, but we nearly lost," I said. "If the police hadn't come in time—" I shuddered mentally. "Eve, you must never—"

"I wasn't going to harm the men," Eve said. "I kept my head. I knew about the ring. I knew if I frightened them

110

enough they would confess. I knew the police were coming. What's more, Adam Link, detective—I knew you were alive all the time. One of your broken cables twitched slightly. I saw that right away." I knew she was laughing a little then. "Poor dear, did you *really* think I had gone berserk?"

Paradoxically, I was nettled. "You mean you weren't ready to—well, avenge me, if I *had* been dead?"

"Now, dear, that's just what you *wouldn't* have wanted—" One word began to lead to another.

Our three friends arose to leave. "Your first quarrel," Jack grinned. "Come on, Kay and Tom. We're excess baggage. And if Eve starts throwing things—"

CHAPTER 15

Alloy Athlete

"I want to file citizenship papers," I said. "I am Adam Link, the robot."

The official, Dahlgren by name, stared at me.

Jack Hall and Tom Link, my friends, stood beside me. Also Eve, of course, my metal mate. We had decided, after long discussion, to try this. Tom had previously sent applications to Washington, but they had been ignored. He had finally said perhaps the best course was the most direct—for me to apply in person at the Federal Building, in this city where I was known widely. So now, I had the complete papers drawn up, with Tom's help, for both Eve and myself.

Our first "naturalization" papers.

"Impossible," snapped the official finally. His face reddened. He felt we were making a fool of him. "Citizenship is granted only to—uh—human beings."

Tom spoke up sharply.

"Can you show me that statement in black and white? The laws read that any *person*, regardless of race, color, creed or nationality, may apply for citizenship. Adam Link is a person."

"Person," scoffed Dahlgren. He looked me up and down with a stiff smile. "It's quite obvious that he's nothing more than a clever mechanical apparatus. A robot that walks and talks. But still a machine. You can't label that a 'person'. What you want is a *patent*."

He did not mean to be insulting. He simply failed to realize that I had human emotions and, above all, a brain.

Eve and I looked at each other. What of our minds? You don't patent a mind.

Tom tried pleading. "Don't look at it that way. They have personality and character of their own, like any of us. They have minds. They think, reason, know the difference between right and wrong. They want to live in our world, as full-fledged members. They've done good already. You know their story—"

He summarized our achievements, and ended with: "You

112

know how they broke up this city's biggest crime ring. Could any humans have done better—or as much?"

Dahlgren gave Eve and me a grudging look of admiration, for that. But he shook his head stubbornly.

"Still, they aren't human beings—legally."

Tom smiled triumphantly, having maneuvered the discussion to that angle. "Adam Link *is* a human being, legally. You read about his trial. He was duly entered in the civil court records. I can furnish them. Also Eve Link, through *her* trial, is legally a human being."

Dahlgren looked as though he had been driven into a corner.

"Technically," he floundered.

"Perhaps," Tom shot back. "But I think it's up to you to prove he *isn't* human—legally. You can't ignore court records. Do you know what Adam Link can do if you refuse to take up this matter? He can sue you."

Dahlgren pondered that, half angrily, half worriedly.

"I'll send the papers to Washington, to higher authorities," he acceded. "I won't take the responsibility myself." He went on, almost spitefully. "I guarantee you they won't accept it. They'll throw it out on technicalities. Where was Adam Link born? Who were his parents? Things like that—"

His eyes narrowed shrewdly then.

"There's more to this than just awarding Adam and Eve Link citizenship, for their good deeds. The question is, do we want *more* robots to follow, parading up and down our streets as full-fledged citizens, accorded all the privileges of the Constitution and the Bill of Rights?"

"What do you mean?" I demanded, and I think my mechanical voice was rather stentorian. "That you think robots might become a menace?"

It was that, of course. Yet, I couldn't blame him for the stand he took. It was, after all, a situation no man had ever faced before, in all human history. Not even Solomon would have seen a clear answer.

I knew the thoughts streaming vaguely through his mind. He was being asked to make room, in human society, for alien robots. For the first of the future robot race. How could he take the tremendous responsibility of that step? How could he be sure some frightful catastrophe might not result?

Frankenstein! A robot race gone Frankenstein! If that happened, he would be blamed. And every official in Washington would feel the same, and shy from the decision.

I had taken a step forward, involuntarily. Dahlgren had paled, perhaps visioning me going berserk. Jack's hand pulled me back.

113

"No use arguing, Adam," he murmured. "I knew this wouldn't work."

Dahlgren stood up from his desk. His instinctive fear over, he spoke directly to me, almost in a friendly fashion.

"I knew you were coming eventually, Adam Link. I've been prepared for this. Do you know what is against you mainly? Public opinion. I've watched the papers. Look at what this commentator says."

He handed me a newspaper, with a syndicated column that reached the homes and minds of millions. I read the item at a glance, with my television scanning:

Adam Link, the intelligent robot, is definitely a national figure today. As a startling, almost fantastic novelty out of some lurid thriller, he captures the imagination. But the novelty has worn off. Even most of the jokes about him have died down.

Science has created metal-life. We can accept that. But we must not blind ourselves to its deeper significance. Adam Link will want to be accepted as a human being. He may have legal status, but so has a dog. A dog may inherit money, and be tried for a crime. And despite his laudable actions so far, and his own protestations that he is human in all but body—*is he human?* I maintain he is inferior to humans in all mental respects. His so-called emotional reactions are all pseudo-human, mechanical, not real. Personally, I doubt if they exist at all.

The commentator, signing himself Bart Oliver, left that damning indictment echoing like a challenge.

"You see?" said the official softly. "A government like ours must never run against public opinion. Washington won't grant you citizenship." Then he waved impatiently. "I'm a busy man. Good day, gentlemen."

He should have added "—and Mrs. Link." He had completely ignored the fact that she was a lady.

Back at his apartment, Jack shook his head again.

"No, I knew it wouldn't work. Not that easily. In Washington, they'll wrangle a while and then reject the application. They won't want to set a precedent, or buck the public. Right, Tom?"

Tom nodded wordlessly, and there was silence in the room.

Tom broke the silence. "Maybe we should take out, the—" he hesitated, glancing at me—"well, the patent."

"No." My microphonic voice was firm. "The secret of the metal-brain is locked in my mind. I would trust no one else with it."

Jack was suddenly fuming.

"That commentator, Bart Oliver. He doesn't represent pub-

114

lic opinion. He just poisons it. Adam Link is inferior to humans, he says like a lordly judge—"

"Perhaps I am," I said. "After all, I'm just wires and wheels. Metal junk strung together. Perhaps—"

But something had struck Jack, forcibly.

"Perhaps, nothing," he interrupted. "There's a way, by heaven. If we can get a tide of public opinion in your favor, Adam, we'd have a wedge in Washington." He looked at me a moment. "Will you let us put you in the public eye?"

Jack went on eagerly. "Sports is what I mean. We'll display your strength and skill in sports. And with it, sportsmanship, determination, and what they call 'heart'. All those human qualities are best brought out in sport activities. Adam, old boy, you're going to make the headlines in a new way. What's today—hah. The Indianapolis Memorial Day Race is next month. I have connections. I'll get you in as an entry if I have to commit murder."

Irrepressibly, Jack made plans. His idea was sound. I would that way win human will and sympathy first, then official recognition.

The Indianapolis racing classic took place.

The jam-packed stands blurred by, hour after hour, as I drove my special car around the oval track. Eve was at my side, as my mechanic, pumping oil by hand to the laboring engine.

We felt supreme confidence in ourselves. In my private car, a powerful one, I had often driven over a hundred miles an hour. I hit 200 here on the straight stretches, and not much less on the curves. I had no worry over a tire blowing out and losing control. Electrons and electricity motivate my brain and body, give me speed and power to a superhuman degree.

There wasn't any competition. I led the field. There wasn't even danger, except when I overtook the racers so far behind, gaining laps. I swung past them one after another, timing the dangerous moments with hairline accuracy. I am a machine myself. Driving another machine is child's play.

"We will win, Eve," I sang above the grinding roar of our motor. "They are so slow and inept, these humans."

"Not all of them," Eve said. "The man in car five—Bronson is his name, I think—has been taking curves faster right along, in the attempt to catch us."

A moment of great danger came. One car skidded on a curve, cracking into another sideways, and both rolled over and over across my path. I was just passing the field again.

There was only a split-second of time. No human could

have avoided crashing into them. Tires squealing, our car swerved for the only opening in the jam.

"Adam! The man—you'll run over him. . . ."

One of the unfortunate drivers had catapulted from his wrecked car in front of me. He might be alive or dead. If I hit him, he would certainly be dead.

The stalled car was in our way. I knew, in avoiding the man, I'd have to take my chances with a collision. When we struck, it was a glancing blow. Any human would have had the wheel ripped out of his hands. My alloy fingers tightened like a vice. The gears of my arms gave a screech of unyielding protest. I held firm. We went on, safely, except for two blown tires.

Stopping in the pit for a quick change of wheels, we went on to win the race, still far ahead. Bronson was second, breaking the track record himself in the magnificent attempt to catch us.

Oil-stained, grimy, so tired he could hardly stand, Bronson grinned at us. "Great race," he said simply. "Better man than I am, Adam Link. You deserved it."

Before the race he had scorned to consider us competition. Some of the other drivers crowding around muttered. Had the race been fair, since I won so easily?

"Shut up," Bronson told them. "We had our laughs before we started. Adam and Eve Link thinking they could win? Hah! A couple of tin monkeys, we called them. We got to take our medicine now. Besides, I saw him take a skid, to miss running over Henderson. Adam Link might have cracked himself up. He takes first money and no beefing."

The crowd had taken the announcement of my victory in a dead, chilling silence. They were hostile. The announcer asked me to say something over the public-address system. I didn't.

I handed Bronson the first-prize check. I didn't need it; we had plenty of the money I had earned as a business consultant in the past.

Jack, on the judges' stand beside me, nodded. "Take it, Bronson. You really won. There isn't a driver on Earth could beat Adam Link."

The crowd burst out in cheers, over this. I knew what it was called—sportsmanship. I had won a point, after all, in my campaign to prove I was worth human status.

Or had I?

That evening, the papers used 72-point headlines. ROBOT WINS CLASSIC. METAL MAN DEMON DRIVER. INCREDIBLE RECORD SET BY ADAM LINK. And more

116

significantly—TIN MAN AND MATE STEAL SPEEDWAY CUP.

Under the latter heading, it said: "Why not run a man against a car? Adam Link was bound to win. It might have been a fairer contest if Adam Link had gamboled around the track himself, machine against machine."

More cutting was the column under Bart Oliver's byline:

Adam Link won the race, but not public acclaim. He tried to, by 'magnanimously' turning over the first-prize money to Bronson. Sportsmanship? I think we all see through it as a spurious act. He was told to do it, undoubtedly, by his manager. Adam Link himself would never have thought of such a human gesture in his cold, metallic mind.

Bart Oliver had appointed himself my Nemesis. I could see that. He was ruthlessly determined to misinterpret everything I did, as so many others had since my creation. But now I had a truly formidable enemy, one who swayed large masses.

I wrote a rebuttal. "I, Adam Link, am a robot, but I have a human mind, not a cold, metallic one. Ever since my advent, certain yellow journals and their paid mouthpieces have dinned against me constantly. The latest is Bart Oliver. I wish to point out that he represents his own opinion, not everyone's, if there is any fairness in human minds."

It appeared in Oliver's syndicated papers, under the heading: "Adam Link's Manager Pens Rebuttal in Robot's Name..."

I will pass over sketchily the many following events. We barnstormed the sports world. In the tennis matches, I won against the highest-ranking player in straight sets.

In golf I achieved a score of 49 on a par-72 course. Three times I drove from one green to another for a hole in one. The rest of the time I landed the ball within a few feet of the cup. An expert golfer takes account of the wind, when he swings his club. But he doesn't see clearly, in his less mathematical mind, a graph showing the exact course the ball must follow through the air. Nor is he able to make allowance, as I did, for the differences in air density as the ball arcs up and then down again.

At a track meet, in an open-air stadium, I ran the hundred yard dash in 5.4 seconds. But Eve did it in 5.3. She is a little quicker than I at the start. I recall the papers playing it up, banteringly, as a reversal of masculine superiority.

We ran the *two*-minute mile. We set a high-jump "record" of 10½ feet, and a broad-jump of 41 feet. In the latter event, we did not dare exert our full powers. When we land our 500 pounds of weight, it jars through our whole mechanism, threatening to disrupt vital parts. As it was, Eve went head-over-heels, cracked her skull-piece against the ground violently, and was "unconscious" for five minutes. I was frantic till she came to and answered the endearments that come as naturally to me as to any man seeing a loved one hurt.

"Is Adam Link really human in mind?" commented one paper over that. "He all but wrung his hands while his metal mate lay knocked cold."

"Another spurious reaction," wrote Bart Oliver. "His 'heart' is an electrical distributor, giving off sparks of electricity, but certainly not of human emotion."

And so it had gone all along, pro and con. Was Adam Link human? Or was he simply a thinking engine? And always the yellow journals, led by Bart Oliver, maligned me. Branded me with such epithets as unhuman, subhuman, pseudo-human, quasi-human, para-human. Never *human*-human.

With his flair for the spectacular, Jack managed to stage an exhibition baseball game, the proceeds for charity. The pitcher for one team was listed as Adam Link, the catcher Eve Link. The rest of our team were minor-leaguers. The opposing team were major-league all-stars.

"Have you ever pitched before?" they asked me.

I shook my head.

"We'll murder you," they predicted boisterously.

I was a little startled till I realized it was part of baseball jargon.

The first man up waited confidently. They knew of my machine-strength, and success in all other sports, but baseball was different. I was against a skilled, powerful team. I sped the first ball down. Too low it was called a ball. The second was too high. The third too wide.

But then I got the idea, and shot the fourth ball straight over the plate. *Crack!* It went into center field. Luckily, it was caught. The second man up watched two of my pitches go straight over for called strikes, then swung at the third. Like a bullet, it came at me and struck my frontal plate with a resounding clang. It might have killed a man. It bounced up from me and came down in my hands. Two out. The batter, having rounded first base, turned back, disgruntled. Any human pitcher would have been forced to dodge the ball and let it go into center field for a hit.

118

The crowd was roaring. Adam Link could be hit. He was not so invincible in baseball as in all else.

The third man up crashed the first ball over my head. That is, it would have gone over my head except that I leaped up ten feet and caught it in my left hand. The first half of the inning was over. The major-leaguers, passing me on the way to field, grinned.

"We'll bust you wide open next inning," they cheerfully informed me. And this time I knew they didn't mean wrecking my metal body and strewing its parts around.

As our side, at bat, went down in one-two-three order, a voice called me from behind the dugout, where I sat with Eve and Jack.

"Jim Brody," Jack explained. "Big betting-combine behind him. He's probably wanting to fix things his way, but we're having nothing to do with that sort of thing."

I shook my head in revulsion as we approached the man. "What do you want?" Jack asked him.

The gambler's beetle-brows were drawn together in a frown. He addressed me. "Look here, you going to win this game or not? The way you're starting, they'll run up a score next inning. And your men won't get a run from their pitchers. Bets have been hard to get except at ten-to-one. If you lose, I'm cleaned."

"So what?" Jack snorted, stalking away.

I thought of deliberately losing, to teach Brody a lesson. But I didn't. The first inning had been experimental. Now I knew the exact range of the plate, the behavior of a ball in flight, the timing of their swings.

I looped my arm around. The ball spanked into Eve's hands almost instantly. I don't think the umpire really saw it, but he sensed it had cut the heart of the plate, and he called a strike. Again the ball whistled down. On the third throw, the batter bewilderedly swung. The ball was in Eve's hands before he even started the bat around. The two following men swung courageously, but belatedly. It was speed they had never seen before.

Thereafter, they went down in one-two-three order, each on three pitched balls. With their slow reflexes, they had no chance. It would be a no-hit game. Eve and I came to bat in the third inning. Swinging experimentally at the first two balls, I sent the third one into the center-field bleachers for a home-run. Eve duplicated my feat. We repeated in the sixth inning, pounding the balls out of the park entirely.

The game was a farce. While I pitched, the men back of me sat and lay on the ground, with nothing to do. They laughed and made biting remarks to the futilely-swinging All-Stars. I could sense tempers flaring. At the end of the sixth inning, thoroughly humiliated, the All-Stars attacked their taunting rivals.

And they attacked me.

"Damned tin gorilla!" I heard, and then bats were pounding at me from all sides. I had heard baseball players were rough and ready men. But they actually had murder in their eyes. splintering their wooden clubs against me. One crack against my skull made me reel.

"Stop," I bellowed. I wrenched a club out of one man's hands and snapped it in half, in my hands.

They all saw. Anger went out of their eyes, and fear came in. They backed away.

"No, I won't touch you," I told them quickly. "But you're poor sports."

"Poor sports," shrilled back one man. "We don't have a chance against you. You've just been showing off your cheap strength, you tin sport."

That epithet was singularly appropriate, from their viewpoint. That was all it had meant to them. Cheap exhibitionism, rather than strength and skill under the control of a humanlike mind. They looked on me more or less as a dancing bear or remarkable puppet, rather than a mental human. I looked at Jack. Our campaign was backfiring.

"Yes," agreed another voice. "You've been trying to prove you're a human being, Adam Link. All you've proved is that you're a machine."

It was not a baseball player who spoke. Part of the crowd had swarmed onto the field. Among them was a slouching figure in a black fedora hat, with a sharp nose and cynical eyes. He stepped forward.

"Bart Oliver," Jack said in recognition.

This was the man who, more than any other, opposed me. Who had taken it upon himself to deny me human status, like a one-man Vigilante Committee. He had led the yellow journals like a pack of wolves after me. I looked upon him as you would look upon a man who tried to run you down with a truck.

He was staring at me with deep interest, his first sight of me at close range. "I came here," he explained, "to look you over. I think it's about time we met. What's your game, Adam Link? What are you after?"

"Game?" I asked.

"Don't act innocent," he drawled cynically. "You've been trying to display human qualities. Why?"

"Why don't you lay off him, Oliver?" snapped Jack. He was warning me with his eyes not to answer.

But I did. I decided to chance all on a direct plea. I addressed them all, players, reporters, crowd. And therefore the world.

"Listen to me. I have tried to show, through sports, that beneath my machine-power are the human things. Eve and I are as human mentally as any of you here or elsewhere. Our kind can be useful, in industry, as thinking machines. As pilots, drivers, laborers, mechanics and in the laboratory. Robots will do only good, never harm. I swear it. But future robots must not be slaves. I am the first of the robots."

I looked around at the intent crowd.

"I want to become a citizen," I finished.

The human faces before me were stunned. It was my first public utterance to that effect. They looked at me queerly, as though the thought were inconceivable. Just as Dahlgren had looked. I suppose the effect was something like a car or animal asking for citizenship.

Bart Oliver seemed less startled than the others.

"I thought so," he murmured. He swung on the crowd too. "Adam Link wants to become a citizens; *and to vote*. Robots can easily be manufactured. Think of thousands, or millions as a *non-human voting block*. See the danger, folks? But right now, and in the first place, Adam Link has not proved he's entitled to human status. I claim he's *inferior* to us in all factors —even *physically*."

He went on to explain his astounding statement.

"Under suitable handicaps, a human will beat Adam Link. Suppose, for instance, that he ran a really gruelling race, like a cross-country run, without stopping for repairs, and with a governor within him to keep his speed at ten miles an hour. Would he win? Would he possess enough determination and courage to stick to his task?"

My phonic voice came out quickly.

"I accept the challenge."

CHAPTER 16

Robot Freaks

Two weeks later, I was at the starting line with five long-distance runners. Eve checked me over carefully. Fresh battery, central distributor sparking evenly, all rivets and bolts tightened, joints oiled. I was ready.

Jim Brody, the gambler, approached us before the start.

"You going to win Adam Link?" he asked me, with all the querulousness of a child.

I answered truthfully. "I don't know. If I break a leg cable I lose under the rule of no repairs."

Brody looked at me speculatively. "I've made some money on you, Link. The odds are ten-to-one that you win, because you won in everything else. Suppose you lost? And suppose I collected ten for one, betting *against* you? I'd make a mint. And you can have fifty percent—"

"Damn you, Brody," I said. It was the first time I'd ever used one of the swear words you humans do. I used it because it was the only way to make myself clear. "I'm going to try my best to win."

He left, with a gleam in his eyes. I knew what he thought—that I would lose. My very choice of words encouraged him in that belief. Frankly, I wasn't sure of myself. It would be a real grind. A marathon. Five hundred miles of rough road. I had never before tested my powers over so long and hard a stretch. I was not made like an automobile, for just such a purpose.

The race started. Within a hundred miles, one of the five men I was racing against had pulled steadily ahead of the field. He was Rikko, a Finn. I kept up with him, at his side.

Four official cars followed. In one rode Jack and Tom and Eve. In the second, Rikko's manager and helpers, with blankets and food. In the third, the official time-keepers. In the last one, reporters and cameramen, and with them Bart Oliver.

By the rules, although I did not need sleep, I had to apportion eight hours out of twenty-four to "rest". During such times I talked with Eve.

"Rikko is running his heart out," she said. We both realized it took a great spirit to run against a tireless machine.

"I must too," I said. "The country is watching. Washington

is watching, Tom says. If I lose, Bart Oliver will have proved his point—that I am inferior to humans. And he will have made us the laughing stock of the world. Our citizenship hinges on the outcome of this race."

Brody approached me when 300 miles had been run. Rikko and I had kept abreast all the time. The gambler had evidently followed in his car. He looked worried. With him were several hard-looking men.

"Look here, Link," he grated. "Our money says you lose. All of it. You better lose—or else."

Once, four gangsters had emptied their guns at me, without effect. "Are you threatening me?" I scoffed. "You forget I'm a metal man."

They left, muttering.

All went well till the end of the third day. The ceaseless jarring and pounding had had its effect on me, but nothing serious. A slight twist on my right knee-joint, making me limp a little. And a tiny short-circuit above my distributor, which manifested itself in my brain as an annoying throb. Pain, you might call it. If the symptoms did not increase, I was safe.

Yes, this marathon was a true test for me. If I won, I would be every inch a champion. The human machine, though weak compared to me, is a marvelously smooth mechanism. It has lasting power. But have you heard yet of a car or engine that can keep up a steady pace without little things going wrong?

The morning of the fourth day, something struck my eye, far to the side. A highway ran at right angles to our pre-arranged course along a country road. A car sped down it. A mile beyond, a train rumbled and would soon cross the highway.

Mathematical distances and measurements integrated instantly in my mind. I saw the car would smash into the train. I swung my chest-plate open, unhooked the governor, and leaped away.

"Adam, you fool—" came Jack's startled yell, from his car behind me.

"Come on, Eve!" I bellowed, as she jumped out. She followed instantly, aware of the impending tragedy.

Together we raced down the highway. The car was doing 80. We did 90, like two metal Tarzans chasing a wild beast. We caught its rear bumper and strained to hold it back. Our 1000 pounds told. The driver felt the drag, saw he couldn't make it, jammed on his brakes. The car screeched to a stop five feet before the locomotive as it thundered past.

Eve and I said nothing to the driver, white-faced and sick now that he saw how close he had been to death. He had learned his lesson.

Returning we found the race stalled. Rikko had stopped to watch and all the others.

"You've broken the speed rule, Adam Link," the racing official said. "I'm sorry, but you've forfeited the race."

"Wait," Rikko muttered. "I don't think that's fair. Let him go on."

A magnificent gesture. Then Bart Oliver stepped up. I saw the gleam in his eye. He wouldn't allow it. He would insist on the forfeit, laugh us to scorn for our mock heroics, kill our chances for citizenship at one stroke.

"Let Adam Link go on," Bart Oliver said tersely. He was looking at the train vanishing in the distance. "That was a 'stunt' that could never have been planned."

Fifty miles to go. . . .

Fifty miles of excruciating torture to me. The strain of catching the car had aggravated the twist of my knee-joint. I had a decided limp. Also my sparking system was worse. Static charges battered within my iridium-sponge brain. I had what in a human runner would have been rheumatism and a frightful headache.

No repairs. No correction. I could only stumble along. Worse, it rained, and all my joints stiffened for lack of fresh grease.

At the last rest-stop, Bart Oliver grinned.

"Have you got a fighting heart, Adam Link?" he jeered. "Jack told me you must be feeling what amounts to pain. Now you know how a human runner feels, with aching muscles and sore bones. And only dogged determination to keep up the grind. Don't think Rikko is feeling any better. He's been running a terrific pace. And grandly. He has a fighting heart. Have you, Adam Link?"

And suddenly, it occurred to me that he was right. Rikko was dog-tired, strained, haggard. He had not said a word. And how much courage it must have taken to pound along hour after hour, trying to beat a machine! Racing what must have seemed a hopeless race, knowing my smooth power.

Fighting heart. *Sisu*, as the Finn himself would have called it. That something in humans that keeps on against all odds, in all phases of life. Did I have it in my mental makeup? I perceived that Bart Oliver was not wholly the cynical human bigot I had thought him. He had put before me the greatest test of my life. The test that would really prove my human qualities—or disprove them.

I kept on, though my "headache" became a crashing roar of static in my skull. My twisted knee jarred through every atom of me, as a sprain might jar a human body with sharp jolts of pain. My stiffened joints called for every ounce of strength in me, to keep up the pace.

I staggered on, rattling and clanking as if ready to fall apart. There was danger of that too. And of the short-circuit intensifying and exploding my whole brain.

The city was ahead, where the finish line lay. Crowds now lined the way, watching the last stretch. Win, win, win!—my mind demanded relentlessly. I could still achieve a sprint and win. But what about the valiant Rikko? He was fighting too, like me.

If I let him win, ignoring what Bart Oliver would do to me, the betting-combine behind Brody would collect an ill-gotten fortune. That wasn't reasonable. There was only one solution. Side by side I ran with. Rikko.

We crossed the finish line in a *tie*.

We both collapsed on a patch of grass, unmindful of the cheering crowd; Rikko panting, sweating, myself grinding internally and sparking with short-circuits at every joint.

Rikko grinned and extended his hand. We shook hands, man and robot. It had been a great race.

Bart Oliver stood over us. He peered down at me strangely. He had been looking at me like that, in the last part of the race, since the train episode.

"You could have won, Adam Link. Why did you make it a tie?"

"As a symbol," I answered. "To show that robots and humans strive for the same goals. To show that Adam Link, champion, is only a man."

I arose, facing him, extending my hand.

"A man?" he echoed. He didn't take my hand. "No, you can't be a man beneath it all. I can't be wrong."

He stalked away, as stiffly as I might have. It had been unreasonable to expect a change of heart in him.

An hour later I was in a machinist's shop, being repaired. I gave the man instructions on what to do. My knee was straightened. The annoying shorts were eliminated and my static headache left.

Jack was jubilant.

"I think we've done it, Adam. The crowd really cheered you at the finish. The man you saved at the train reported the incident. 'Adam Link for Citizen', a lot of them yelled. I don't think even Bart Oliver and his gang of human snobs can turn the tide. Bart Oliver is furious. He has been shown up. Other papers are laughing at *him* now."

Adam Link for Citizen! Was it rising, a swelling chorus that would reach the ears of Washington?

The proud day came, only a week later. A huge shining limousine pulled up at the hotel in which we had a suite.

"A Congressional committee wishes to see you, Adam and Eve Link," said the driver. "Your citizenship is ready to be granted."

Jack and Tom stepped forward with us, but the driver held up a hand. "Sorry, only Adam and Eve Link, the robots. It is a special closed meeting."

We all stared at one another. "Odd," said Jack. "Why all the secrecy? Something about this is funny. . . . oh well. Washington always does things the hard way. Good luck, Adam and Eve."

The car delivered us and we were ushered into an inner chamber of the Naturalization Bureau. Senator Willoughby was there with five distinguished men, three in uniform—an army general, a navy admiral, and an air-force general.

I glanced at Eve puzzled. What were military men doing here? What had they to do with our citizenship?

Willoughby cleared his throat, as if to make a speech. "Adam and Eve Link, we'll get down to business quickly, granting you citizenship. I am sure all the people of this country will consider it a just reward for your exploits. You have been in the nation's eye for some time. You are—to put it simply—nationally known figures."

My metal chest does not expand under praise. But I think my body straightened a little. After all, I was only "human". I felt proud and happy. At last people were treating Eve and me as equals. But strangely, I noticed that Eve did not seem elated. She was staring fixedly at the military uniforms.

"We have the papers all made out," Willoughby went on smoothly, sliding them toward us. "By the way, on top is a simple form for you to sign also. Just a formality. Then you receive the citizenship papers. Please sign the form first. Adam Link."

I grasped the pen. In another moment I would be Mr. Adam Link, United States Citizen. I wished Dr. Link, my creator, could be beside me at this fulfillment of his dream.

I paused. Eve touched my arm. Her low whisper came to me alone. "Adam, the men in uniform are leaning forward. Are you sure everything is all right?"

Men in uniform—

Cold water seemed to splash over my mind. I picked up the form on top and read it, for the first time. Words shocked their way into my brain.

Be it hereby agreed, by Adam Link and Eve Link,

Naturalized Citizens of the United States, that since they are given full human status, they are also privileged to serve in the armed forces of our nation. And in view of the present international emergency, Adam Link will agree to immediately build more robots, which will then be used to. . . .

I did not have to read any further. I laid down the pen quietly, sadly. I had been about to sign myself into military slavery.

"A mere formality—" Senator Willoughby began, but there was guilt in his voice. Undoubtedly he himself had been forced to try to sign me up.

"Formality?" I said in low bitter tones. "No, gentlemen. I cannot sign. I cannot allow robots to be used in human warfare—*ever*."

The military men glanced at one another. "But after all," spoke up one, "along with the privileges of citizenship, you must also take the responsibilities. All other citizens are willing to fight for their country if need be."

I faced them, the three men in uniform. How could I make it clear? "I consider this my country as much as you do, gentlemen. I would never be disloyal to it, in any way. But as a robot, I have a greater duty to *all mankind*—never to allow robots to become a *menace*."

I let that sink in and continued. "Please see my side of it. Robots must only be servants of peace—as workers, builders, engineers, scientists. They must never take human life. Or else one day"—I shuddered a bit and went on—"one day there would come the terrible struggle of all robots against all mankind."

I went on in this vein for some minutes. The men fidgeted. They had lost interest. The military men arose and left, flatly. I was just a soap-box orator now, talking of things that were annoying and thought-provoking.

Willoughby stopped me, his face a bit pained. "You would be useful to us in the armed services. If you do not accept that condition, we cannot grant you citizenship."

Eve and I stared at each other, dazed. Our great moment, for which we had strived so long, had come to this. Most likely, with citizenship, Eve and I would instantly be called into military service. Commanded to build an army of robots. That was our only use to them.

I was reduced to begging, clutching for a fading dream. "Let us show our worth as workers, laborers, scientists. Anything but warriors."

Willoughby turned away, biting his lips. I could see how distasteful this all was to him too. One of the other officials

127

spoke up, his face set, voice stony. "Sorry, Adam Link. You can have citizenship only with immediate conscription. Take it or leave it."

Eve and I turned away. It was our only answer. Robots must never—NEVER—take human life. I turned back for a last word to them, these men who only saw us as a new tool for war.

"I will show you how robots can be of benefit to the world, without fighting your wars."

Promise? Or vain boast?

CHAPTER 17

Calling Adam Link

A warm July evening found Eve and me alone in our isolated Ozark home, talking over the adamant prejudices humans held against us. I felt dreary, soul-sick.

"Eve," I was saying, "we're done. We're finished. Everything we've tried in the world of humans has failed. Our chance of becoming citizens now—sunk without a trace."

"Don't say that, Adam," Eve said. "We'll prove our worth yet."

"We have no worth," I grated. "Except as a few cents worth of junk. We're intelligent robots, but we're of no earthly use whatsoever." I repeated the bitter self-denouncement. "We're of no earthly use whatso—"

Interruption came, in the form of a knock at the door.

We started, looking at each other. Who was visiting us? Who had taken the winding, little-known road leading to our door? A pack of humans, perhaps, to once and for all rid earth of robots?

"Don't resist," I told Eve. "I suppose it had to come to this —our extinction."

I flung open the door. There was no pack. There was just one human—a man with hat pulled low, one hand resting in a pocket as though gripping a pistol. He gave me a glance, darted his eyes around the cabin, then stepped in. Back in the shadow was a car in which he had arrived. He had an air of profound secrecy.

"Adam Link?" he asked quite unnecessarily. I cannot easily be mistaken for Frank Sinatra.

"Yes. Who are you?"

For answer, he drew back the flap of his coat, displaying a small medallion, whose inscription he explained.

"Secret Service of the United States. I am Joe Trent, Operative Number 65. We want you, Adam Link."

"Official lynching?" I hissed, and suddenly my brain smoked with rage. "Go. You humans won't finish me off this easily. Go and come back with all your army. You'll have to blast me out of the hills if you want me."

I would go down in earth history as a one-man rebellion,

holding off a mighty army for days and weeks. They couldn't deny me that last flash of glory.

"You refuse?" the Secret Service man said.

I nodded grimly, waiting for him to threaten me with all the forces of the army, navy, and air force.

Instead, his shoulders seemed to sag a little. His voice changed to pleading.

"You don't understand," he cried. "We're in trouble. Washington's in trouble."

I stared.

"In trouble? You mean you've come to ask my—help?"

He nodded eagerly.

"I've been sent here by the—"

Breaking off, he went to the door, peered out cautiously as though fearing eavesdroppers, then closed it carefully. He turned back. What was the need for all this elaborate secrecy?

"By the President himself," he finished. "We need you, Adam Link. You're our last hope. We're stumped, and we've come to you as the last possibility to avert what may be catastrophe for our nation."

"Explain," I demanded, half dazed.

"First of all, I must swear you to utter secrecy. None of this must leak out to public channels. Have I your word?"

I nodded. At his hesitation, I added, "I never lie. That is a human trait." He took that without argument, and went on in a rush.

"The story is this. A month ago, a certain destroyer of the United States fleet passed San Domingo on routine patrol. San Domingo island is our possession, as you probably know. The captain saw a strange thing on the headland—a new fort. The fort had not been there a month before. It had not been commissioned by our government. Whose fort was it?"

"Obviously that of a foreign power," I put in. "They sneaked it in right under your noses."

The operative shook his head.

"Impossible. Our fleet regularly patrols that area. It would take a whole convoy of supply ships to put up such a fort. No convoy could brazenly sneak through our naval lines."

"Then they dropped the material and men from the skies by aircraft," I said impatiently. "Or by rockets."

"That's what we're afraid of," Joe Trent nodded. "Natives at the other side of the island reported seeing a great lighted ship come down one night. It meant that a foreign power had established a foothold in our hemisphere."

"So what?" I snapped. It seemed so childish, these human doings. "Since you discovered the fort before they operated from it, it's simply a matter of destroying it."

130

"We tried," Trent responded. "The destroyer shelled the fort when it refused to answer by radio. We had the right. It's our soil. The fort seemed unharmed. Other ships came to try, including heavy cruisers. They shelled it with the biggest guns known to naval science."

He paused and went on in a whisper, "Not one shell took effect. Not one chip was knocked off that fort."

My impatience vanished. This was really something.

"You suspect what?" I asked.

"The worst," he groaned. "A certain foreign enemy—I need not name him—has established himself in an impregnable base from which to operate against us."

His face went haggard.

"You're the last hope, Adam Link. We thought of you when all else failed. You have a super-brain, some say. We don't know. Can you help us?"

How can I describe the overwhelming thrill that shot through my iridium-sponge brain? Humans sought my help. They had hounded me, balked me, sneered at me. Now they begged at my knees.

Should I refuse? Should I send him away, as they had so often turned me aside? What did it matter to me whether one group or another of humans ruled here? But suddenly a horrible picture flashed in my mind. Regimented robots under the command of a hard, ruthless regime. Their leader would not ignore me. He would *use* me—in frightful ways.

"I'll try to help," I said. "Where do I go?"

"Thank Heaven," Joe Trent said. "Everything has been arranged. I'll take you in my car to the nearest airport. A plane is waiting there to take us to Key West, one of our naval bases. At Key West, a warship will take us to San Domingo."

"Come, Eve," I said. "We will look over this mysterious fort that cannot be destroyed."

Why did I agree to help at all? I who had once before refused citizenship itself, because it meant taking part in war. I explained it to Eve, privately.

"If the enemy attacks America and wins, he will then rule the world. The very first thing he would do would be to *force* us into his military machine. We would have no choice. In free America, we still have the choice itself. That, Eve, is worth fighting for."

Eve nodded. "We will not help America, or any group of humans, to *conquest*. But we must save America, if we can, from attack and defeat."

Forty-eight hours later, the cruiser X steamed in the night to the headland of San Domingo island. In the grey dawn, a fort slowly took visible form on the coast. I was on the bridge with

131

the captain, the fleet commander, and Joe Trent. All the warship's crew were at guns and battle stations, ready for any attack from the fort.

"There it is," Trent said in nervous tones. "It's within missile range of the whole eastern seaboard. It must be destroyed."

I looked the mysterious fort over. Even from our distance of five miles, the closest they dared go, the fort loomed like a mighty man-made mountain. Through binoculars, it was a dome-shaped structure with a solid rampart of metal facing the sea. From recessed apertures bristled ugly cannon snouts.

The world does not know of this—any of this.

And now, the final assault was tried. A co-ordinated attack by land, sea and air. This had been in preparation for a month, since the fort was discovered. The other attacks had been preliminary.

First the naval forces hurled over tons of shells, from their extreme range behind dense smoke screens. One little crack in the dome might mean victory. At the same time, the air force bombed relentlessly, from high up.

Then, at a prearranged time, the barrage ceased, and the waiting land forces attacked directly. They came at the back of the fort, from the island's interior. Tanks formed the spearhead, rumbling forward with spitting guns. Behind followed shock troops. If the stupendous shelling and bombing had opened one little crack, one means of entry, they would invade the fort and finish the battle within.

From our observation plane, we saw a strange sight. A barrage from the enemy shattered the first line of tanks. They simply blew to bits. The second wave roared up—to the same fate. The third and last line of tanks gallantly charged—and stalled. Stalled dead, as though their crews had fallen asleep.

It was the same with the shock troops. It took magnificent courage to charge, against what they had seen. But I suppose they were filled with a blind rage at this maddening enemy.

Three waves of men tried to crack the nut. Two waves went down like mown grass. The third wave fell, but limply, as though gassed or paralyzed. And then the rest of the soldiers, their morale finally broken, fled in complete rout.

I saw one more thing, before falling dusk obscured vision. Figures scurried from the fort, carrying the limp men in, as prisoners. And the undamaged tanks were driven inside, with their unconscious crews.

Three days later, after night evacuations of all natives, the ultimate weapon was tried. But when the nuclear mushrooms of hellfire cleared away, the mystery stronghold smote our eyes—undamaged.

The battle was over.

You will find no record of this, I repeat. There could be no official declaration of war, since the enemy had not yet been identified. I think the sunken ships have been ascribed to sabotage for public consumption.

"The fort is absolutely impregnable," Trent moaned. "Now the enemy can hack away at America's defense lines at its leisure."

He looked at me.

"This is where you come in, Adam Link. Our human methods have us stumped. Are there any methods you, as a robot, can try?"

I shook my head, and Joe Trent wept. Yes, he wept. For he knew that his country was doomed.

"Adam," Eve said sadly. "Isn't there anything we can do, as robots?"

There was still faint hope in Trent's hollow eyes.

But I shook my head again.

"Trent," I said. "Advise the government to send one tank of marines up to the fort. Have it fly a white flag. It will be a commission to ask the enemy its terms."

"God," Trent said hopelessly. "I guess you're right. But suppose they ruthlessly destroy the tank—and go on, wishing complete invasion?"

"I want to go with the tank," I said. "Eve and I, disguised as humans. If they destroy the tank—" I shrugged. "If they let us in to talk, fine. You see, I want to get *inside* that fort."

Joe Trent stared.

"There's one method left," I finished. "Sabotage—by robots."

It was daybreak.

One tank, a huge monster, rumbled slowly toward the back of the fort. From the conning tower waved a large white flag. There were six humans in the tank—to the casual eye. Two were the crew, one at the controls, one at the guns. Two men were high officials whom I cannot name, empowered to receive and deliver the enemy's terms to the United States government.

The remaining two were Eve and myself. Again, as once before, I was disguised as human. Eve also. Flesh-colored plastics hid our metal bodies. Skillfully molded pseudo-features gave us the appearance of two rather stocky, poker-faced thugs. Eve was a "man" too. The disguise was a deception that might not hold up more than an hour or so. But I wanted to get within the fort. Once inside, I would see what could be done.

But there was the chance that the enemy would simply annihilate us.

"If that happens, Eve," I murmured to her. "Farewell. Our

133

short sojourn among humans will be over in a flash of unsung glory." .

"Goodbye, dearest," she returned, against that eventuality.

The humans with us in the tank were grim, pale. Would the enemy receive us? Or would they blast us to atoms, so that there would be no excuse for not going ruthlessly on, invading the continent?

Our answer came with one swift sweep of the scythe of Death. The universe split open in a rending crash. The tank crumpled like a cracked walnut. A second shot exploded within, flinging the riddled bodies of six dead humans out like broken debis.

No, four dead humans.

Two of the original six flew fifty feet through the air, landing among bushes with a metallic clang. Eve and I should have been killed, too, except that after the first shot we had leaped with snap-reflexes. We were already sailing out of the split tank when the second shot hit. Its concussion merely blew us into the bushes.

To the enemy, it must have seemed we were destroyed, too. Well they knew no human beings could survive those two direct hits. They were right. No humans could. But Eve and I, with hard metal beneath our false human disguise, were no more than shaken up by the concussion and the hard landing on the ground.

Still, we lay stunned, hardly aware for a minute that we were alive. Dents were in the metal beneath our human clothing, from flying pieces of the shattered tank. But we lived.

I moved my mirror-eyes and saw Eve lying ten feet away, flat on her back. Her hand twitched as she was about to spring up, happy to be saved.

"Hsst!" I whispered. "Don't move. Let them think we're dead humans."

Thus we lay still. We were in full view of the fort. If we moved the slightest, they would see it. But it was simple for us to automatically shut down our internal locomotor center. We were then "dead" from the neck down. We lay as completely inert as any corpse.

We lay that way all day, motionless.

The enemy did not come out. They let the bodies there to rot, as all the troops they had slaughtered lay rotting further back. The utter heartlessness and brutality of the enemy enraged me. They must be monsters at heart. I felt like springing up again, denouncing them in stentorian tones.

But that would be sheer folly. We must wait for night, get in the fort, and fulfill our mission. Fate had lent us a finger, so far.

Night fell at long last. When the deepest darkness had arrived, I signaled Eve and we cautiously arose, hiding behind bushes.

No light hung outside the fort. And no light shone from any aperture or window. They had built the fort as solidly as a half-shell of steel set down squarely on the ground. Certainly it was the queerest structure we had ever seen or heard of.

I estimated its dimensions from its bulking curve against the star-filled sky. No less than a half-mile in diameter, and 2000 feet high. Colossal engineering had been required to erect it. They must have worked on it months and months. Yet Joe Trent swore it hadn't been there a month before.

I shrugged.

"Let's get in, Eve," I whispered. "I want to meet these amazing humans who have done miracles in engineering and warfare both."

Get in, but how? Sheer blankness of wall mocked us. I strode close to the structure, in shadow, and rapped on it slightly. Metal? But it gave no ring, only a dull thud. Not wood, certainly. Some kind of plastic, harder than steel? It must be harder than tungsten-steel, to withstand all the bombarding I had seen.

"With bases like these to work from, Eve," I said, "they can easily conquer all earth. This must be a long-range plan by dictators to rule the world. We must get in and spike this place some way. *Any* way."

But we stood baffled before the adamant structure.

Fate again leaned our way.

We threw ourselves flat as a sudden glow fell around us. Had we been spied? But then I saw the light was only a reflection bouncing down from some greater light at the dome's peak. This light shafted like a searchlight beam straight into the sky, with an intensity that drilled through scattered clouds. It must be visible for hundreds of miles.

"I see," I told Eve. "It's a signal beacon for their supply and reinforcement ships across the ocean. One or more must be due to land."

A moment later, a giant aircraft dropped from the sky, of an advanced design I had never seen before.

It dropped almost noiselessly as if the motors, too, were of a new design superbly muffled for swift, silent work. It landed like a VTOL or helicopter, not a hundred feet from where we crouched.

At the same time, amazingly, one whole section of the dome soundlessly raised, like the flap of a tent. The ship trundled in, with scarcely a whir of its mysterious motor.

Two robots trundled in after it, with scarcely a whir of *their*

135

motors. It was the chance we had been waiting for. We were inside.

We scurried to a corner of the dim hangar, flattening against the wall like two motionless shadows.

I congratulated myself, but too soon.

Radiance burst through the room, as some central light clicked on. The glare revealed us plainly. Half-blinded, we noticed figures stepping from the plane. They were facing us. They could not fail to see us up against the bare wall.

Worst of all, the pitiless glare would reveal the imperfections of our human disguise. And the blasting of the tank had knocked off bits of our plastic faces, further exposing us. The enemy would know us instantly for robots, and probably destroy us as dangerous. Our mission was nipped in the bud.

Hopelessly, I looked around the hangar. The huge sliding door had shut fast, sealing us in. No other door was open. We were caught. Yes, we could run around, kill those here if necessary, but the rest would know then with whom they dealt. They would besiege us in this room. A fair-sized gun would blow us to bits with a direct hit.

Trapped. Our only hope had been to get in and seek hiding before we were seen. Now, with this light on, and no egress from the chamber, we were caught.

My eyes suddenly ceased looking for escape.

They turned back to the figures, whom I had given but a glance. A picture was transmitted from my eye-mirrors to my brain that jolted me much more than the tank explosion had.

In fact, I refused to believe what I saw. I told myself that something had gone haywire with my mechanical optic center. Perhaps a wire loose, or a short-circuit throwing everything out of balance. For what I saw just didn't make sense. It was a hopeless distortion.

Yes, it must be that. But then, why was Eve staring rigidly, as though she had seen a ghost?

I clicked shut my eyes, looked again.

This time I knew it was no mistake.

Eve's startled gasp came to me.

"Adam!" she said. "They aren't—aren't—"

"No, they aren't," I agreed dazedly. "They certainly aren't!"

And they weren't.

They *weren't human.*

CHAPTER 18

Robots vs. Aliens

Imagine first a gorilla. Then an upright buffalo with horns. Then a surrealistic statue representing a hunchback on whom a mountain has fallen. Blend the three together—long powerful arms, horns at the top, hooves at the bottom, a bulging torso with the head set forward, and the whole thing nine feet tall. Ugly, brutal, repulsive, horned Goliaths.

Oh yes, it was *manlike*. That is, it didn't have extra arms, or two heads, or tentacles, or any other distortion of that kind. It had two legs, two arms, a body, one head with two eyes, two ears, and one mouth.

But all the primates, and most mammals, are built in the same plan as man. Yet there is endless variety. These beings were as different from man, in a horrible fashion, as a gorilla. They walked upright and used their hands for manipulation. From there on, their similarity to man ceased. They were alien —utterly, nightmarishly alien.

Even I, a robot who was no more than a grotesque parody of man in metal, felt closer to human than these monsters were.

And suddenly the whole aspect of this event changed to something appallingly ominous.

"They aren't human," Eve was still whispering. "Adam, what does it mean? Where are they from?"

"I don't know," I returned dazedly, still stunned. "I don't know, Eve. They're not of earth, that's certain."

Eve abruptly gave a sigh.

"Well, It isn't a foreign invader after all. Won't they be surprised and relieved to hear that, outside?"

I think I felt like striking Eve for the thoughtless words.

"Relieved?" I grunted. "Good Lord, Eve! Don't you get the significance of this? This isn't a mere earthly power invading the Western Hemisphere. No, nothing as simple as that. This is a race from another planet, come to take earth from *all* humans."

Eve digested that, trembling.

"What shall we do, Adam?" she breathed.

I stiffened.

Three of the aliens had stepped from the ship, turning to-

137

ward us. They saw us, now. Their hands leaped to holsters, drawing out a mechanism not unlike a gun. They strode forward, covering us.

"Don't move, Eve," I warned. "We don't know how powerful those guns are."

They approached with a ponderous step on their hooved feet. Heavy and solid they must be, far heavier than a human, and far stronger. Yet they walked with a certain mincing step that indicated earth's gravity was trifling to them. Their home-world must have a tremendous gravity, like Jupiter.

Were they from Jupiter?

I wanted to ask, but naturally they had an alien tongue.

The foremost horned giant eyed us with green-irised eyes. He towered three feet above us.

"Two more of the earthlings, eh?" he said in perfect English. "How did you get in? Don't be so startled. We tuned in your radio, upon arrival, analyzed your language and learned it. We have need to talk with you—what do you call yourselves?—oh yes, humans."

Humans! He took us for humans. To his inexperienced eyes, our half-messed human guise was as good as gold. He saw no difference between us and the previous captives. Humans were new to his eyes.

Instantly, I played that advantage up, giving Eve a quick glance.

I spoke, but I didn't say—"yes, we're humans." That was taken for granted. In fact, it would have aroused their suspicions. I simply recounted how we had sneaked in after the plane.

"For what purpose?" the alien demanded, then answered himself. "To spy on us, of course. You hope to escape with your information. No prisoner can escape. We will keep you alive. We will have use for you, either for vivisection or mental study."

He turned. "Mog, take them to the prison."

I pondered in lightning thought.

I could charge them, at this moment, and take their guns away before they could shoot. I need not fear their obvious strength as a true human must. But to resist now would expose us immediately as robots. I would have little chance to find out more about them, the fort, and their plans. Better to remain prisoners for a while, and take our chances with them later.

I let my shoulders slump, for Eve's benefit. She caught on quickly, making no move to resist. The being named Mog prodded us with his gun toward the other end of the hangar.

Again it was almost humorous. Any human, poking us with his gun and meeting unnatural hardness, would know us for robots. But Mog, having poked few humans, did not know they should all be uniformly soft.

But humor left me as we strode along.

These non-terrestrial beings represented a stupendous threat to earth. Their mighty fort, their superpowerful guns, their easy efficiency in learning English, added up to super-science.

Eve must be thinking the same as I. If only this *was* a foreign but earthly enemy invading America. Better that than this—invasion from space.

And outside this dome lay the world—unknowing. Unaware that soon they would be battling for existence with a foe ten times more powerful and unsympathetic than any human aggressor.

Opposite the dome-door, in the hangar, was another door that now opened. Several other aliens appeared from the interior. At their head was one who by his manner and dress must be a high official, perhaps chief of the whole dome.

I haven't mentioned clothing. The aliens wore extremely light clothing, merely shorts and a belt with all else bare, as though to them earth climate was tropical. Moreover, it occurred to me that the dome was air-conditioned. I could not feel it directly like a human. But my compensating thermocouple, that allows for extreme temperatures which might tighten bearings, had swung to its low side. The temperature in the dome must be about freezing.

The chief wore a broad chest band with insignia on it, and the others saluted him by touching one hand to their horns.

Our guard, Mog, began to address the chief in their native tongue, but the chief interrupted.

"Use the English tongue, Mog, for practice. It is the earthlings' most important language. We will have much need for it later. Now, who are these two?"

"Two humans who sneaked in after our plane to spy, Chief Thorg. I'm taking them to the prison."

Chief Thorg gave us his attention. For a moment, at his sharp stare, I thought he had penetrated our disguise. Then he laughed—or what I took for a laugh. It was a sort of whistling wheeze.

"These little humans," he said, "come in all assorted shapes and sizes and disfigurements. Look, this one has no nose."

He pointed at me, and I realized with horror that somewhere my plastic "nose" had been knocked off. Was he playing with me, knowing our deception?

"Where did you lose your nose?" he queried.

"In a war," I improvised hastily. "It was shot off."

And the Chief swallowed that! He was already shrugging. He addressed Mog again.

"Your report?"

"We sailed through the stratosphere of this planet, over what I believe are called Europe and Asia continents. A short flight on this pygmy planet. Dropping low at times, we saw their cities and centers. Very backward there, as everywhere else on this world. There was some kind of battling going on in one place, I believe. It was hard to tell, as they fight with such puny weapons."

"Yes, they have puny weapons indeed," the Chief agreed. "Their clumsy attack, the other day, with iron tubs in the water, slow little aircraft, and paper-thin metal carts on land. They are apparently in the Metal Age." His tone was derisive. 'Stone Age', he meant. "It seems they know nothing of plastic science and atomic hardening. Well, we will soon conquer them. Take the prisoners away, Mog."

Mog prodded us through the door and down a long corridor. We passed various other aliens. The dome must be crammed with them. Had they all come in one spaceship or several? Were more spaceships arriving regularly, augmenting their forces for the grand day of victory?

Those were things I had to find out. I felt a little crushed already. One lone pair of robots against a dome full of these invaders from the void. What hopeless odds faced us?

I tried to pump Mog.

"How many of you are there here on Earth?" I asked.

"Quiet," he growled. "Speak only when you're spoken to, prisoner."

A side corridor branched to the large prison room. The wide face of it was simply a series of open bars. Behind the bars were the human prisoners. A hundred or so of the soldiers who had been gassed in the battle I had seen.

The jailer unlocked the door. Mog shoved us in.

"Join your fellows," he laughed. "And talk over the end of your race's rule on this planet."

Eve and I stumbled forward in the rather dimly lit prison. The men hardly glanced up, haggard and despondent. They sat or sprawled on the cold stone, shivering and suffering. We had stumbled over a corpse laid by the door. The jailer dragged it out without a word, locking the door again.

"Pneumonia, I guess," chattered one man to us.. "Died an hour ago. The tenth one already, that way. Welcome to hell, strangers."

I inadvertently stepped on his toe, in the close-packed chamber.

"Ouch! Damn you—" He was suddenly a wild, enraged animal, his nerves broken by the cruel imprisonment. He cracked his fist against my face—or tried to. Eve caught him by the shoulders and held him as easily as a child.

His rage gusted out in stunned incredulity at Eve's strength. And he was suddenly peering at us closely. All the men were.

"Why, you're not—not humans," he gasped.

Others had jumped up.

"It's the damned aliens in disguise! Tear them apart—"

"Stop, you fools," hissed another voice. "Can't you see the metal in spots? It's Adam Link the ro—"

"Shut up," I snapped quickly, shaking my head violently for their benefit. "I'm Adam Link, the spy."

They caught on, especially when the jailer appeared at the bars. "What's the commotion in there?"

Silence greeted him and he left with a shrug. He hadn't heard the near giveaway. It was my sole ace-in-the-hole, to be taken as a human by the enemy.

I made my way to the far corner of the prison, out of earshot of the jailer if we talked low. The men quietly moved around me.

"Adam Link the robot," breathed the man whose toe I had crushed. "I'm Captain Taylor, chief officer of these men. Are you with us, Adam Link? Maybe with your help we can break out and do something."

I was a little gratified that they had heard of me and my exploits. Most humans had ignored me, or passed me off as a freak or clever toy. These men accepted me as an equal, and sought my help. I cut off these personal ruminations.

"When the time comes," I whispered. "Right now, I have some questions. You were gassed, before capture?"

"Couldn't have been gas," the captain returned, puzzled. "I had my men wear gas-masks. We saw, heard, and felt nothing. All our muscles just suddenly went limp, as if paralyzed. We didn't lose consciousness. The effects wore off in a few hours, after we were locked up here."

Induced paralysis? Perhaps by a projected, invisible ray. My heart sank. Another manifestation of their advanced science. Whole armies and cities rendered helpless, captured without a gunshot, if they wished—

Captain Taylor was suddenly moaning a little. He was, after all, a young man. Recent events had been soulshaking.

"God, the shock of it—seeing these inhuman beings. Horrible creatures from another world. It's a wonder we aren't all insane. Poor Jones did go. I put him out of his misery myself. Adam Link, we've seen enough to know the whole world is threatened. We've got to do something if we can."

"Easy," I said at the hysterical edge in his voice. "We can't go ahead blindly. What else do you know?"

141

"Mighty little," Taylor muttered. "We've been locked up in this ice-box all the time. They feed us from the kit-rations they picked up among our dead, after the battle. Every day a few have been taken out. They don't return."

I knew what happened to them, but didn't tell Taylor. Vivisection and mental study. Humans put under the knife and microscope, like interesting little bugs, so that the aliens would know every factor of the race whose world they wanted to wrest away.

Taylor knew nothing of the layout of the dome, or the number of aliens, or their guns—things I had to know. I pondered.

"You have a plan?" Captain Taylor asked hopefully. "Somehow I feel glad you're here, Adam Link. You've got to save the human race."

All their eyes turned to me. I was already accepted as their leader, their champion. Champion of the world, of the human race. Within me, a wild elation surged. It was good to have humans accept me at last, place their trust in me.

But still, what could I do?

"For the present," I began, "we will wait—"

Interruption came as the door grated open and three aliens stepped in. One of them was Mog again.

"We want three of you—any three," they announced.

They grasped the nearest three men by the arms, roughly, and began dragging them away. One shrieked, struggling to escape. He jabbed his fist in Mog's face.

The giant jabbed back. His gorilla-like arm delivered a blow that knocked the human cold. Then the alien bent the limp form across his broad chest and slowly began cracking its spine.

"I am strong," Mog boasted. "Watch, as I break this wretch in half. It will teach you others a lesson."

The other men watched in helpless horror. Some turned to me in appeal, but they knew I did not want to reveal my identity. It was more important to save earth than save this man. I told myself that, for about one second. Then I acted.

"Adam, don't—" Eve hissed, grabbing my arm.

"Let go, Eve. There are some things—"

I was there in two strides. I caught the alien by the arm, wrenching him around so that he dropped his burden. Mog glared down at me, from his height of nine feet. I was David before Goliath, a little pygmy scarcely reaching to his chest.

"You must want a taste of my strength," he roared, pounding his fist into my chest. The blow knocked me back a full inch. I was amazed, for never before had any creature short of another robot displayed such power.

142

He struck again, but this time I was braced. He gave a grunt of pain as his arm went numb.

I struck back, full in his ugly face, but only succeeded in staggering him a little. I was again astonished. The blow might have snapped the neck of a human. For my second blow, I used fully half my machine-power. My arm shot out like a steam-piston. The alien flew back against the iron bars with a thud.

He came roaring back to finish the fight, but now I saw the folly of my course.

"Cover me, men," I yelled.

They understood. They milled about me so that I was lost in their numbers.

"Which one was it?" demanded Mog angrily. "Which one of you weaklings thinks he is stronger than I. Where is he?"

But luckily he couldn't pick me out by sight. The light was dim and it had all been a swift blur of action. All humans looked as alike as peas to them. His two companions pulled him back and calmed him down.

"Let him go," they admonished, half laughingly. "Next time don't pull your punches, Mog. Now we'll take our three."

They pulled their holster weapons this time, aiming at three men. Only a slight buzz sounded from the instruments. The three unlucky victims fell limply, all their muscles paralyzed. The three aliens carried them out, and the jail door clanged shut.

"Thanks, Adam Link," Captain Taylor said simply, as some of the men attended to the victim I had saved. All the men looked at me, half in awe at my strength, half in gratitude.

"Forget it," I said. "I nearly gave myself away. I'll have to be more careful." I resumed where I had left off, before the interruption. "For the present we will lie low and—"

"Lie low?" Captain Taylor suddenly blazed. "While earth is doomed if we don't do something? While they take us out one by one, cutting into our numbers? No. If you haven't a plan, Adam Link, I have. Next time they open the door we'll rush out in a body, fight our way through—"

"How far?" I asked sharply. "You humans are brave—but fools. How far would you get against an unknown number of them? And what is the way out? And what powers their guns? And what is their dome made of? And how many more spaceships are coming? And how can this dome be sabotaged effectively? We have to know those things, instead of blindly rushing out to become corpses who died in foolish glory."

"You're right," Taylor muttered, subsiding. "But how are we going to find out? You can't get out of this cell to do any spying around."

"You forget who I am," I said without boastfulness. "There is only one kind of jail that could hold Adam Link. A completely solid steel chamber—if the walls were thick enough. Now be quiet all of you."

It was late night now in the outside world. And in this dome, the hum of activity floating down the corridors died gradually. The aliens slept at night too, fortunately.

I watched the single guard on duty outside our barred room. He was sitting in a chair-like support, leaning against the wall, bored at the thought of his all-night vigil. Gradually his eyes blinked and closed. Sounds rumbled from his barrel chest. He slept.

"Now is my chance," I whispered to the men.

"How will you get out?" Taylor queried.

For answer, I strode to the bars where the ends were buried in the cell wall. Bracing my feet, I tugged at a bar. My locomotor unit within hummed as rising horsepower fed into it. I kept an eye on the guard, but he slept heavily.

The bar was thick and strong, more resistant than any jail bar of earth, which I would have jerked away with one hand. Eve had to help me. Together, like metal Samsons, we bent the bar. It came away suddenly, out of its socket. We loosened a half dozen more, forming an aperture wide enough to slip through.

The soldiers had watched with silent wonder. I faced them.

"Stay here. Too many of us would invite detection. Eve and I will scout, since we are the swiftest and strongest. We will try to be back before the guard awakes. Come, Eve."

A moment later we stood beyond the bars, in the hall. We bent the bars back into place. Even if the jailer woke for a while and looked around, he would not know of the two who had skipped.

Before we stepped away, I held Eve back against the wall.

"Photoelectric units across the front here," I warned. "To announce any jail-break. Hug the wall carefully, and we won't break the beam."

Cautiously, we slid sideways for twenty feet. Beyond that, the beams did not stretch. We were free. We strode silently down the corridor. It was dimly lit, as were all the passages during the night-period.

At the next cross-corridor, I paused. I pondered as to the general lay-out of the honeycombed dome.

"That searchlight," I told Eve, "must shine up from some room at the apex. We'll try to find it."

After several turns, we came upon a passage whose floor sloped upward steadily. It was the one we wanted. We crept along like two metal ghosts, warily watching for aliens. One appeared, abruptly, a guard lounging on routine duty. From his niche shone a patch of bright light we would have to cross.

He was not asleep, though staring vacantly. We would have to distract his attention. Estimating the curve of his niche, I made a tiny clicking sound. With mathematical precision known only to a robot-brain, I knew the sound would reflect in an acoustic curve back of him.

He started, came to his hooved feet and turned, wondering who or what was clicking in the wall back of him. While he thus surveyed the blank wall, Eve and I tip-toed across the lighted patch and melted into the shadowy stretch beyond.

Not long after, the slope led us to what I calculated must be the center of the dome. I was sure of it when it opened out into a gigantic round chamber. There were lights burning within and aliens were at work. We hugged the doorway's shadow.

I ran my eye swiftly around. The room had a sliding roof, now closed, like the sliding roofs of astronomical observatories. In the center was a huge bowl-shaped object, surrounded by what seemed to be generators and other power-producing apparatus.

The signal-light.

From here, rolling back the roof, they shone their super-searchlight, guiding their scout craft back from all corners of a world as yet new and not fully mapped to them.

My quick, searching eye noticed two other things.

One, that large recesses leading off from this giant room held the ring of defense guns.

Second, and more arresting, there was a huge unfinished machine at one side. Workmen were on scaffolds around it. Somehow, with huge crystalline tubes and a maze of wires, it suggested a radio. A transmitter, perhaps, with which to signal their home-world, hurling radio waves far into space? It must be important to them, since this was a night shift at work.

We watched one workman. He was completing a framework, enclosing a great tube. A tubular, hissing affair in his hand sprayed out smoky matter that instantly congealed to form the hard construction beams. It was miraculous, like forming something out of nothing. And forming something harder than steel, for it was the same material of the dome.

"How is it done?" Eve marvelled, in a whisper camouflaged by the noise they made. "They seem to draw it out of no-where."

"From the air," I said. "They are masters of plastics. They draw oxygen, nitrogen and carbon dioxide from the air and compress them instantaneously into dense plastics, ten times harder than polyethylene or any metal, earth is just exploring plastic science."

"How fast they work," Eve said. "It's almost like a spider spinning out his web as fast as he can move."

"It accounts for the rapid construction of the dome," I nodded. "Joe Trent swore the dome was not here a month ago. They built this whole dome in that short time. Any comparable structure would take earth engineers at least a year. Let's look at the guns, Eve."

CHAPTER 19

Robot Saboteurs

Following a passage that led to the gun-emplacements, we approached the first. Dark and unattended, we could make little out except that it was surprisingly small—a mere ten-foot instrument of intricate design. But the guns must be super-powerful. They had shot earth warships out of the water, with one charge each.

By what principle? What did they shoot? How did they aim so accurately?

The answer came more quickly and completely than I wanted.

Without warning, an ear-shattering report sou ded against the outside of the dome. Then I caught the drone of aircraft. The U.S.A.F. was making a desperate night attack, since the truce attempt—the false one Eve and I had been part of—had come to nothing.

The aliens streamed to their guns. What I saw then I hardly believed. Each gunner simply wore a helmet with wires trailing to the breech of the gun. Then he raised his eyes to a plane above, seen through a slit, and the gun magically aimed the same way. Finally, at his silent command, the gun spoke only a fractional second later. The target plane exploded into debris, struck by a hissing charge of something infernal.

After watching this same performance a few times, it all clicked in my mind. "Eve," I whispered. "Earth has no chance against that weapon. It shoots electric bolts at the speed of light itself. And most diabolical of all is their aiming method—simply looking at a plane with their eyes. The most accurate 'gunsight' possible. And a simple swift thought-command then fires the gun. In essence, the aliens kill with their thoughts. Aim, fire! Aim, fire! As fast as they *think* it, humans die."

After dozens of American planes went down, the attack broke.

Stunned, Eve and I returned to prison, bending the bars straight after letting ourselves in. In the morning, the awakened dome would not know of the two robot spies who had learned much—but not yet enough.

147

"What was the excitement about?" Captain Taylor asked. "We heard muffled thumps down here."

He and his men listened to our story with incredulous eyes.

"Thought-controlled guns," Taylor mused. "If we could spike those, the dome would be defenseless—"

"For about a week," I cut in. "Earth forces would continue to bomb—and fail to chip off an atom. And in a week, the aliens would make new guns with their plastic magic. No, men. We have to get at the *root* of the dome. Somewhere they must have a generator that feeds power to the guns. Probably a thermonuclear unit. If I can find that . . ."

The next night, Eve and I again sauntered out of prison. Again our jailer was sleeping away a watch that to him seemed totally unnecessary.

We roamed completely around the dome, looking for a central power-plant. We peered in bunk-rooms, in which aliens slept heavily. Supply rooms, stacked with boxes and plastic-cans of their food. The air-conditioning room, where a huge, silent machine piped cold air, normal to them, through the dome.

"If we could only find a room with weapons," I told Eve. "Distributed among the men, we would have an armed fighting force."

But there seemed no small-weapon supply, outside of those carried by the aliens themselves. Balked at every turn! We could not keep up this night spying forever. Sooner or later we would be discovered. Before that, we had to have some definite plan of action.

I reported no luck to the men, back at prison. They groaned in dismay. Each day several of them had been taken away, never to return. Our numbers were going down steadily. And the chill of prison was weakening those left.

"We've got to do something, Adam Link," Taylor kept saying. "Can't you think of anything?"

He was beginning to lose faith in me. All the men were. They expected Adam Link, from stories they had heard of me, to storm through the aliens like a metal tornado. They could not understand my slow, cautious course.

They did not know that Adam Link was afraid, for the first time in his life. That for once he was up against powers that appalled him. That even a robot must hesitate before things of nearly equal strength, ability and science.

"Patience," I admonished. "Nazi Germany was not pulled down in one day."

The third night Eve and I explored all corridors leading down. Finally we found it—the power-room. But it was completely sealed off. Diamond-hard plastic walls barred us.

We could only put our ears to the solidly locked doors and hear within the low, steady hum of the generator.

"Probably supplies a hundred gigawatts to the guns above," I said. "Namely, 100 billion watts, a magnitude unknown on earth. Those guns blast like lightning, at a pressure of at least 10 megavolts. This plant could probably light half of the world for a year. There is more power concentrated under this dome than in all the cities of earth combined."

"But we can't get at it," Eve murmured. "We can't spike it."

"No, not yet," I agreed, filing the room's location away in my mind. If we could find some instrument or method of breaking into the power-room, it would be the answer.

We found another corridor winding down. It opened out into what I knew must be an underground space. It was wide, huge and dark. We did not make out the bulk in the center at first, till our eyes adjusted to the gloom. Light strayed from the corridor.

The object was 1000 feet long, 100 feet wide, in a torpedo shape. It had no wings. From front and rear projected tiers of tubes, many fanning downward.

"It's their space ship," I breathed, "with which they dropped down on earth like a striking eagle. Let's look it over."

Undisturbed, we spent an hour there. Its hatch was open. The hull was empty, except for its motor. It had brought the aliens, all their supplies and equipment. It was stored away now, not needed except in the remote event of having to flee.

My scientific curiosity was feverishly aroused by the engine. Was it a thermonuclear powerplant, spitting atom energy from the multitude of drive tubes? How far had it propelled the mighty ship through space? At what stupendous velocity?

I examined the machine with awe. No engine on earth approached it. Autos, trucks, trains, ocean liners, jets, crawled over earth's surface at a snail's pace. Even orbiting satellites at 17,600 mph, and space probes at escape-velocity's 7 mps, could not come near this starship's fleetness. Their stupendous craft had plunged through the deeps of space at perhaps fractional light-speed.

"Eve," I exclaimed. "Now we're getting somewhere. If I could once find out how to run this ship—"

How did it operate? But here I was completely stumped. The science of earth was dumb before it. The science of Adam Link stammered in bewilderment. The control board was an electronic maze of switches, relays, dials, rheostats, all numbered and designated with the alien's enigmatic figures.

"Only the aliens could tell us how to run it," Eve said. "And of course that's out of the question."

149

Ironic situation. A plan was shaping in my mind. A plan to demolish the dome. But one vital factor was missing—how to run this ship. And certainly the aliens wouldn't oblige to their own undoing.

"Still," I growled impotently to Eve, "we could wreck the thing."

"What good would that do?" Eve said. "Except to make them all the more determined to conquer earth, having to stay."

Another thing caught my eye, in a dark corner of the huge underground hangar. A dully glinting angular shape of metal. A tank. One of the captured tanks that they had driven in, perhaps for examination of earthling war-machines. A pile of metal back of it told of the other tanks taken apart in the investigation. This one tank was left, probably as a museum-piece after earth had been conquered.

"That tank, Eve," I whispered. "It has guns, ammunition, armor-plate—"

Eve shook her head. "One tank and two robots against a dome-full of aliens?"

The odds were still against us. We turned away and slipped back to prison.

"Any luck?" Taylor asked hopefully, for his shivering, miserable men.

I shook my head.

"I still don't know how many aliens there are, altogether. That's vital. Tomorrow night I'll try to get a count on them. And plan a course of action."

"Tomorrow night," Taylor groaned. "Always tomorrow night. And each day six of us are taken away, one or two die from sickness, and we all go slowly mad."

"Patience," I said wearily. "Tomorrow night I promise you a plan."

And then, as though to smash my careful course, aliens came that day.

They ran an eye appraisingly over our ranks, picking the three burliest men. Two were six-foot men, weighing over 200 pounds apiece. I was the third. I had tried to escape being picked, hanging back as before but this time they singled me out. I was, in appearance, a sturdy human being.

"Come along," said the aliens, waving their guns. "If you don't come willingly, we'll paralyze you."

The two men shrugged, waved farewell, and stepped out without a word. I followed, without a word. There was nothing else to do. If I resisted now and exposed myself, it would be too soon. Perhaps, before they were done with me, I would find out vital information.

150

I signaled Eve with my eyes not to worry about me.

We were led up the sloping corridor that I knew. It led to the apex of the dome, into the giant chamber of the signal-light, gun-recesses, and unfinished transmitter.

Workmen were just clambering down from the scaffolds around the latter. A space had been cleared and roped off, near the searchlight. Chief Thorg stood in the center, where we were stationed, and his men congregated around.

"You have been working hard, men," he said, still using the English language. "Our schedule has gone well. Now, as reward, you will have some other sport, since the earthlings have given up attacking. Our best fighter will battle three humans at once."

It was a sport arena. . . .

A half-naked alien strode up. It was Mog, with whom I had exchanged blows once. By sheer coincidence we were again pitted together. How could I fail to show my true strength this time? It would probably be a battle to the finish, like the Roman gladitorial affairs of a past age.

The arena cleared. Mog, an ugly, overgrown, horned monstrosity, swung his long arms and prepared to tackle us three. The spectators cheered, urging him on.

I swept an eye around, counting the aliens. Nine hundred and ninety-three, perhaps the dome's full force except for a few at watch-stations below. One thousand of the extra-terrestrial enemy, a formidable number. I filed the fact away in my mind. It was a vital factor and the final one—almost.

But now, what about Mog?

The battle was short, ghastly. The two earthmen bravely met Mog's charge, even running to meet him. Mog punched one to insensibility, with rapid blows, while the other clung to his arms futilely. Then he took them both by the scruff of the neck and cracked their skulls together. He dropped them, and faced me.

I had hung back. Yes, I had let the two men die. Yet I had had to silently yell to myself that more than two lives were at stake. The world was at stake. Three billion lives. My duty was clear, under these grim circumstances. I had to learn one more thing about the dome. I had to keep my human subterfuge. When Mog came at me, like a lumbering behemoth, I grasped him around the middle and hung on. Wildly he hammered at my back with his huge fists, but only wore himself down.

The watchers tensed. Who was this human who had hung back like a coward, and now seemed able to take any punishment?

"Oh, it's you!" Mog roared, finally recognizing me. "The strong one. I'll show you—"

He stooped and gave me a bear-hug, in return. His knotty arms squeezed with force that would have crushed every rib in a human body. It actually made my rivets squeak a little, under the plastic disguise and clothes. I couldn't resist squeezing back, taking care to measure out the force of it sparsely. All his breath came out, in a gust. His eyes swam dizzily.

I let him get his breath back, but thereafter he was weakened enough so that his blows came fewer. He kicked at me with his hooves, and gritted his teeth at the pain of nearly breaking his leg. He tried picking me clear off the floor and dashing me flat. I put my foot-plate back of his knee and he very nearly wrenched his own arms out.

"Enough," Chief Thorg said suddenly. "You are weakening, Mog. This earth air is thin. Too much effort might harm you. You have furnished us sport. Now back to work, everyone. Guards, take the earth prisoner to the vivisection room."

From bad to worse!

I had successfully come through the match, unrevealed as a robot. Now they would "vivisect" me. One thrust with a knife and they would know—

What now? Challenge them? Run and hide? I might have tried the latter, if there weren't so many present. But they would be after me like a pack. No, I would have to take my chances in the vivisection room.

The vivisection room, somewhere below, was a grisly place.

Human corpses, in various degrees of dissection, lay on slabs. On one slab, a poor wretch was still alive, his naked body covered with incisions and gore. I steeled myself. No use trying to save him. He was too far gone. If I killed the alien torturer, the mangled human would die anyway a few minutes later.

The victim squirmed against his straps, gave a week gasp, and expired. I relaxed. A robot cannot show it, but within me I was sweating in rage and pity.

My turn was next. Methodically, I was strapped to a slab. Questions were hurled at me, first. Mental inquisition, for useful information.

"How many of you earthlings are there on this planet?"

"Guess," I returned contemptuously.

"How many cities on earth? Where are the important ones located?"

"Here and there."

"Which is your weakest continent?"

"The one called Atlantis," I lied.

152

The alien glared, and lowered his horns, butting me in the side. I think he nearly broke his neck. He didn't try it again.

"Stubborn, like all the rest," he growled. "Well, I'll take you apart now."

He wrenched my clothes off.

"Peculiar specimen," he commented, bending over me.

I was. My plastic disguise was badly battered, both from the tank explosion and Mog's manipulations. Metal peeped forth here and there. And instead of my nose there was only a gaping hole.

The alien biologist peered up and down. Surely he must see. Any moment he would yell his discovery, that I was a robot. Then I would be forced to act and quickly—and still without a definite plan.

But he made no yell. His unaccustomed eyes still took me for a strange variety of the human specimen. Some had been scarred, being soldiers by profession. This one was scarred more, that was all. I almost laughed in his face, calling him a fool mentally.

With quick efficiency, he wheeled an apparatus over that I knew instantly for an X-ray machine. He snapped a button several times, taking full-length prints of my interior. How amazed he would be to see the developed prints—wheels, wires and cogs. But that would not be for hours, perhaps. I had gained that much time, if he did nothing more to me.

But now he poised a gleaming knife over me.

"This will hurt," he said bluntly, emotionlessly. "We are studying the nerve reactions of you humans under pain, for future reference."

He plunged the knife down. He made an incision in my chest under the skin—or plastic. I squirmed, and gave a microphonic moan for his benefit.

He nodded, as though it checked with previous reactions. Again he incised what in a human was a delicate, painful nerve. Again I squirmed. But the farce could not go on. Had he forgotten that human bled when punctured?

I calculated my chances, preparing to spring up.

He jabbed the knife again, deeper this time. It met metal with a jar. Startled, he drew the blade out, staring at the blunted tip.

I sat up, snapping the straps like strings.

"Now you know," I said. "I'm a rob—"

I was interrupted. A voice droned from a loudspeaker set in the ceiling.

"Our radio has just contacted Ship Two, which is now approaching the Solar System. Leave all posts and come to the

Apex Room. Chief Thorg wishes to outline further plans, now that Ship Two is known to be coming."

The aliens in the dissection room looked at one another joyfully.

"Ship Two is coming," one said. "It will be good to see some more of the fellows from home. Let's go. We'll take this prisoner below."

I was safe for the time. The alien biologist was too excited to remember his bent knife now. They conducted me below, to the prison, then left.

The prisoners gathered around me eagerly. I was the first one ever to return, from the unknown horrors above. Eve touched me in the way I knew meant she was mentally sobbing in relief.

"How did you get back alive?" Captain Taylor asked. "What did you find out?"

I told the story. They clenched their fists, hearing of the brutal death of the two men in the arena, and shuddered at the horrible end of the vivisection victim.

"Murder," Taylor hissed. "Plain stark murder and torture. And you didn't stop it, Adam Link?"

Suddenly they all drew away from me a little. I had let the tragedies occur right under my eyes, without lifting a finger. Humanly, they resented it.

"I couldn't expose myself," I said patiently. "I must continue to parade as a human, and find out one more thing."

"Yes—find out how to escape," one of the men piped up loudly. "It's clear now, Adam Link. You're afraid yourself. Afraid of being finished off, once they know you for a robot. All you're thinking of is your own safety."

Another soldier's voice rang hoarsely.

"I wouldn't be surprised if Adam Link was thinking of going in cohoots with the aliens. After all, Adam Link isn't human either, and——"

"Shut up," Captain Taylor commanded. But the protest was weak. He too was looking at me askance.

I was under suspicion. In one moment, in their confused human minds, I had changed from champion of the human race to deserter of the human race.

What could I do or say?

For a moment I wanted to shout at them angrily. For a moment, too, I began to wonder if this human race were worth saving, with all its ingratitude, twisted psychology, and fool distrust.

But I spoke quietly.

"I will have to try to prove now where my loyalty lies. But

it must be in my own way. I must know one more thing, before I am ready to act against them."

I strode to the bars and looked out into the hall. No guard was there.

"Now is my chance," I said. "They are all gathered in the Apex Room, above, at conference. We'll go there, Eve and I, to eavesdrop."

The men said nothing as we slipped through our usual aperture after a moment's work, and stood in the hall. We angled past the photo-electric beams, which was always a tricky job.

"Safe," I breathed to Eve.

At that moment, like a thunderclap, a bell clanged. The alarm! The next second. I heard bells clanging all through the corridors of the dome. How had it happened?

CHAPTER 20

Battle for Earth

"Look," Eve cried, pointing back. "The men followed us, and ran into the photo-electric beams."

The soldiers were streaming out of the prison, as fast as they could wiggle through the opening I had neglected to close. I had not meant to come back to prison this time. The men congregated in the hall, ready to plunge for victory or death.

"Fools," I yelled. "You've ruined everything."

"Think we were going to stay and die like rats?" Captain Taylor yelled back, face twisted. "You were going to join the aliens. Your whole idea in coming to this dome was to contact the aliens and make a pact with them against the human race."

I was stunned by the fantastic accusation.

"You didn't even give me the benefit of the doubt," I groaned. "And now what are you going to do, with the aliens marching here?"

"We'll, at least have a fighting chance," Taylor growled.

But they didn't.

The aliens were already in sight, coming swiftly down the corridor from above. They drew their guns, seeing the escaped prisoners.

"Come on, men," Taylor called the charge. It was magnificent bravery—but a bravery that deserved no respect. He took five steps, and crumpled to the floor, paralyzed. His men surged forward in a wave, and went down in a wave.

The aliens stood in a phalanx, spraying their paralysis-ray in the narrow passage. As fast as the front men fell, those in back were exposed and fell. In a short ten seconds, the whole human force lay limply on the floor.

It was a symbol of how easily the enemy from space could defeat all earth, when they swept out.

The abortive jail-break was over. All the humans were down. The aliens had won. There was no one to oppose them.

No one? There were Eve and I. . . .

It suddenly came to their notice that Eve and I still stood. The paralysis-ray had washed through our unfeeling metal bodies harmlessly.

Eve looked at me. This was the moment.

We were the champions of humanity. Eve waited for me to bellow the challenge, trample them down, and battle the rest in the dome. The men in back waited, conscious though helpless. It had come to this—two mighty robots at last coming from behind human skirts and crushing the cruel raiders from the void.

They waited, as seconds ticked by.

But I did not bellow the hopeless challenge.

My thoughts were curious, for such a moment. The bitter episode in the prison was still etched like acid in my metal brain. Champion of humanity? Of a humanity that had scorned me since creation, reviled me, called me Frankenstein? For them I should battle these formidable beings. These beings from another planet who might, for all I knew, *respect* me.

Yes, curious thoughts. Still, what was there to do? No matter how frightful the odds against me, I must fight.

I tensed to spring. The head alien, Mog again, was aiming a different weapon, larger and more deadly looking. He would try this more destructive force against the strangely-standing two. I did not bellow a challenge—and warning. I would have to leap with deadly, silent speed, in action swifter than their reflexes.

But Mog was hesitating, looking me over closely.

"Wait," he grunted. "It's the noseless one again—the strong one. Who are you? You displayed strength near to mine, in the arena. And now, you stood up against the paralysis-ray, as no human does."

It clicked in his mind.

"You are not human," he finished.

I tensed again. Knowing me for a robot, or at least a non-human, he would kill me the quicker.

Again he hesitated, pondering.

"While we were running up," he mused, "we heard you shouting. You were quarreling with the humans. And one of the humans said something about you two coming to our dome only to join with us. Is it true?"

I thought a long, burning, wondering second.

Then I nodded.

I looked at Eve. Did she understand what went on in my mind in that eternal, blinding second? She did.

"Adam," she gasped. "You're deserting the human race?"

"Why not?" I snarled. "You saw a moment before how they turned against us."

Mog was watching us narrowly, not quite certain of his own deductions. Finally he circled us, while his men kept us covered. He stood over the fallen Captain Taylor.

"Are those two of your human race?" he asked. "Are they your friends?"

Taylor could not speak, with a paralyzed throat. But the flash of hatred and denial in his eyes were answer enough.

"Come," Mog said, looking at me as one strong being to another. "This is very, very interesting. I will take you to Chief Thorg."

Chief Thorg received us in the Apex Room, where his short conference was already over.

Mog reported the jail-break incident, then eagerly told of his discovery.

"More than one intelligent race on this planet?" Chief Thorg said, surprised and thoughtful. "I thought myself you seemed somehow different. You are a race entirely different from the human?"

I nodded. I did not want him to know, for the time being, that we were robots, *created* by the human race, and owing it basic loyalty. Nor did I want him to know there were only two of us in existence.

"Race," he had assumed. That is, a race of other *biologic* creatures. It fitted in with my new decision.

Eve read my thoughts, as she always does, with uncanny accuracy. If robots were presumably to have a place alongside the alien victors, Thorg must think we were a numerous and powerful group of people, without suspecting we were metallic robots.

The aliens, I knew, were realists. They would kill us off simply as dangerous rivals, if they had the chance. Therefore, an intimation of force would result in compromise.

But Eve shrank from me a little. She clutched my arm in appeal.

"We cannot desert the human race, Adam, even if they hate us. This is their world, and our world—"

"Nonsense, Eve," I snapped. "There can be no truce between our species and humans. Ever."

Eve gave up, and nodded.

"You're right, Adam. We would be fools to hope to patch up things with the humans. If only humans had not resisted us with such blind, backward, superstitious stubbornness. They made our lives a bitter struggle against ignorance and stupidity."

Thorg listened to our tete-a-tete with sharp interest.

"I take it the human race hates your race. They had tried to exterminate you? How many of you are there?"

"We are not as numerous as the humans," I bluffed. "But we are far stronger, and hold our own easily. We have atomic-

158

weapons. More than once we decided not to exterminate the humans, as we easily could have."

"A little soft-hearted," Thorg scoffed. But behind that was a deep respect for our avowed power. "You are scientific?"

I waved around.

"This dome is made of stable, polymerized chain-molecules, compressed together so that they touch, isn't it? It is far stronger than porous metal. We have a weapon that can pierce it—vibration."

Thorg started. The deductions had struck home. He was visibly impressed. By what I left unsaid, he could only assume that our "race" was able to resist humans—and the aliens too.

"Perhaps your people and mine can make a pact?" Thorg said cautiously. "Will you help us defeat the humans and enslave them?"

At that moment, I felt that the universe held its breath.

The decision was plain before me. When Captain Taylor and his men heard of this, they would surmise what went through my mind. Joining the aliens meant a complete reversal of loyalty. Champions of the human race we had been an hour before. Betrayers of the human race we would be now, if we accepted. The aliens were realistic-minded. They would give robots a place alongside them, on conquered earth, realizing our worth and special abilities. They would not label us Frankensteins.

Humans had rejected me and my coming race. These aliens wouldn't. The decision was plain, and Taylor's men would analyze in their minds why I made the one I did.

"What are your terms?" I asked.

"Complete and equal mastery over humans, along with us," Chief Thorg answered. "Definite terms will be agreed upon later, according to what parts of this planet you control, and what help you give."

"Good enough," I agreed. "As emissaries of our race, we will come to terms. But first, tell us who you are, where you are from, and what your plans are."

Thorg's story was strange and impelling. Again I have no proof of it. It will ring falsely, fantastically, to your stunted human minds which still arrogantly believe that in all the mighty universe, only earth was given life, and only man was given intelligence.

Eve and I waited breathlessly to hear his story. Only days before, we had stepped out of the normal world and into this dome. With shock, we had laid eyes on the first alien beings ever to visit earth. Curiosity consumed us, as to their origin and history.

159

"With your great strength, you must be from a larger planet," I said. "Such as Jupiter."

Thorg shook his horned head. "We are from the star I think you call Sirius."

Eve and I absorbed the wonder of that, beings from a star-sun's planets lying 50,000,000,000,000—50 trillion—miles away.

"It is only logical that you are not from our own solar system," I returned. "Jupiter is frigidly cold, and probably has no breathable atmosphere. The other planets are likewise ill-adapted for life. It's likely that of all suns with a family of planets, only one or two have the right conditions to support life."

Thorg gave me a glance of respect for the deduction.

"Sound reasoning," he said. "Our sun too has a family of planets—twelve. Only one supported life—our planet Korlo. Perhaps 25,000 of your earth years ago, our race achieved civilization and science. We passed through the Metal Age more than 10,000 years ago, the Atomic Age 5000 years ago. Now we are in the Subatomic Age, manipulating matter and energy at will.

"A hundred years ago we achieved spaceships, and colonized all our planets. Then, very recently, we cast our eyes out into the great void, swarming with stars. Our destiny lay out there, building an interstellar empire."

I nodded to myself. Intelligence is restless. It ever seeks new worlds to conquer.

"Nearest to Sirius lay this sun with a family of planets," Thorg resumed. "Powerful telescopes resolved the satellites, and this expedition was launched."

"Sirius is eight and one-half light years away," I said. "How long did it take you to arrive?"

"Seventeen of your years," Thorg informed. "Since we achieved half the speed of light."

Seventeen years in space! Eve and I marveled not at the time, but at the speed. Building up a velocity of 93,000 miles a second was no small feat.

"This has all been a great adventure," Thorg continued, his saturnine face lighting up. "Two other ships were previously dispatched to earth and were never heard from again. Either their engines failed in space, or they struck large, wandering meteors. This is the first ship to arrive. But now that the trail has been blazed, others will follow."

He pointed to the great searchlight.

"This was built as a signal-light for our scouting aircraft, which we brought disassembled. But also for Ship Two to land near us. Two starships were sent on this expedition, a month apart. If one failed to arrive, the other might. But both won through without mishap. Ship Two is passing Pluto now. We will shine the light tonight. Ship Two will land beside the dome."

"Only two ships were sent to conquer earth?" I asked dubiously. "The humans are many. It might take years to beat them into submission."

"We realize it is not a small job, though assured for us," Thorg returned. "No, not just two ships. Now that we have successfully arrived and scouted earth, plus additional earth data Ship Two will help us gather, the main forces for conquest of your world will follow in due time."

He pointed toward the giant transmitter, which busy workmen were hurrying to completion.

"It will be finished tonight, too. Then a message will be hurled back to our home planet."

"It will take eight and one-half years to arrive," I pointed out.

"One hour," Thorg contradicted. "This is our long-range radio. It will project impulses through the sub-ether, at almost an instantaneous rate. The message will reach Sirius in an hour, telling of our success. Then a waiting armada will be dispatched. A hundred more ships. With these reinforcements, we'll conquer humanity overnight, when they arrive."

It would not be for seventeen years. But in that time, these first arrivals would consolidate their position, and scout earth until they knew every city and gun and factory. When the time came for action it would be an overnight conquest.

"Good," I said enthusiastically. "I see you have laid sound plans. I am glad to ally myself and my race with you of Sirius. You are making interstellar history. You are a great race. Bridging the void alone is a mighty achievement. The human race does not even have one starship, only a few manned experimental spacecraft."

"Would you like to see ours?" Thorg said proudly. "Come, I'll show it to you. But first—"

Without finishing the sentence, he led us to the prison room.

"We are realists," Thorg said bluntly. "I need proof of your pledge to our case. Mog, bring out a human."

Mog unlocked the prison door and pulled a man out by the arm. It was Captain Taylor.

"Kill him before my eyes, Adam Link," Chief Thorg said.

I looked around. The tableau seemed to freeze. Thorg and Mog watched me narrowly, to see if I would kill the humans I avowed were my enemies. The men in the cage stared in frozen silence. Eve turned away a little. For all our new alliance, it would not be an easy thing to do.

161

Stonily, I strode to Captain Taylor. I placed my two hands around his neck, slowly squeezing. That would be best, strangulation. But I hesitated.

"Go ahead, Frankenstein," Taylor taunted me, without flinching. "Surely the life of a mere man isn't going to stand in your—"

I clipped off the bitter denunciation. I squeezed. Taylor's face went purple. A moment later I dropped the limp body.

Chief Thorg clapped me on the back.

"You're with us all right, Adam Link. Mog, throw the corpse back in prison, so that the humans can mourn over their leader. Come, Adam Link. I'll show you our spaceship."

When we arrived at the underground hangar, I did not tell Thorg that I had seen it once before. He might wonder why I had spied first, before joining him. I did not want our newly-formed alliance to be riddled with useless, unimportant suspicions. And that I had been the thankless champion of humanity.

Workmen were there, just starting to dismantle the ship.

"Since we contacted Ship Two," Thorg explained, "we have no need for this ship, for emergency. We are getting rid of it. This underground chamber will be converted into barracks for the new arrivals."

He conducted us through the ship, explaining its various features.

"The space trip was not easy," he continued. "Acceleration for a year produced a terrible ache in our bones and organs. Then, coasting for fifteen years, we had little to do but think back and think ahead. One man went mad, and was exterminated. Then deceleration for a year again. Arriving on earth, we were half dead.

"But recuperation was quick, in earth's light gravity. Our world is about Jupiter's size. We are used to three times more gravity than this. We feel light as feathers here. And it makes us proportionately stronger, far stronger than humans."

He was looking at me suddenly.

"You are strong, too, as Mog found out. Are you stronger than we are?"

"Perhaps a little," I laughed. "Tell me more of the ship. It intrigues me. How does the engine operate?"

"Thought-control," Thorg answered briefly. "As with our guns."

I glanced at Eve ruefully. Before, looking at the intricate engine, we had wondered how it operated. We had not thought of the mental-control, though that was so obvious.

A group of workmen passed us, approaching the engine.

"Careful while you dismantle it," Thorg warned them. "It

has its own power-plant. Energy is still in the coils. Mog, you go and turn off all the switches first, so there won't be any accidents."

I glanced at Eve again. Power was still on, in the ship. If we had known that when first seeing it, and guessed at the thought-control, we might then have accomplished our original mission. But that was while we were still champions of humanity.

"I've wanted to ask you a question, Thorg—" I began, when a messenger came running from above. He thrust something in his chief's hands.

"What is this?" Thorg asked. "You are from the dissection room. Why are you so excited?"

"These are X-ray prints," the other Sirian gasped. "They show—"

He held them out mutely. The prints would speak for themselves.

I knew what they showed. They showed a seemingly human body, lying flat, all its insides revealed to the X-ray's penetrative eye. They showed wires, wheels and cogs.

I tensed as Thorg began looking them over. What would his reaction be, knowing us at last for robots? Beings more alien to him than even humans?

"My question is this, Thorg," I went on imperturbably, as though ignoring the interruption as something unimportant. "If you failed to send the long-range radio message back to Sirius, would the follow-up armada come anyway?"

"No," Thorg said abstractly, looking over the prints with a puzzled eye. "Receiving no message, our people would assume we had been lost. Sending these ships is a costly proposition. They would give up coming to this sun at all then, and try some other star."

"Thanks, Thorg," I said. "That's all I wanted to know."

"What?" he said, still absorbed in studying the prints. Suddenly his eyes blinked, as the significance of the X-rays struck home. He looked up.

"You are a robot," he accused. "A mechanical being."

"Indubitably," I agreed. I went on rapidly. "You wanted to know how strong I was before. I'll show you—*now*."

My fist drove into his face, with all the power of a machine behind it. Thorg's giant form toppled over backward, turning three somersaults, his horns and hooves alternately clacking on the floor.

"The engine, Eve," I yelled. "Before they touch it."

Mog and his workmen had turned at the swift, bewildering attack on their chief. There were twenty of them. Twenty of the towering giant monsters between us and the engine. They

163

stood only a moment, as Eve and I bore down on them like express trains. Then they jerked out their guns.

The paralysis-rays went through us harmlessly. They had forgotten. But now Mog, aware of their uselessness, had drawn his other weapon. It was the one unknown factor left. Would it blast, like their cannon, blowing even metal to atoms?

"If he gets one of us, Eve," I told her swiftly without slackening pace, "the other goes on. You know what to do—"

Eve nodded.

Mog fired. The electrical bolt leaped to my body, with an impact that made me stumble. But it did no more than knock plastic off and scorch the metal. It was a hand-weapon designed to blast human flesh, or Sirian flesh, but not hard metal.

Mog stared in disbelief, as I came on unharmed. Then he fired again and again, blindly, at both of us. The other Sirians too. Bolt after bolt ripped into us. Our plastic burned and melted away.

One shot tore away my artificial ears and lips and hair-wig. My true metal face shone forth.

It takes long to tell this. But it was only seconds while we leaped toward them in great bounds. I try to imagine at times how profoundly astonished the Sirians must have been. Two seeming humans coming at them, changing under the blasts of two gleaming, powerful monsters of metal.

"Robots," one of the Sirians screeched. "Intelligent machines—"

Then I was among them.

I cracked the first one on the skull so hard he sank without a groan, dead. I snapped the second one's neck with one sledge-hammer rabbit punch. I grabbed two necks, and cracked their heads together, flinging the limp bodies aside. Giants they were, half again taller than I was, but I pulled them down to my level for blows. Eve was beside me, punching with the rapidity of a rivet-hammer. And with all its horsepower.

It was a grand fight. A soul-satisfying fight. With each blow, I hissed the name of one of the prisoners who had gone to the dissection room. With each death, I counted one earth plane pilot paid for.

CHAPTER 21

Adam Link, Citizen

Giants they were, hulking monsters of incredible strength. But they had no chance. Their blows against us served only to break their arms. They kicked viciously with their hooves, and howled in pain as the ankle-bone went numb or snapped. They stooped and butted with their short, wicked horns, and succeeded only in stunning their brains.

In turn, Eve and I butted with our metal skulls, often with enough force to cave in a chest with the muffled sound of cracking ribs.

Eve and I were at last exerting our full mechanical fury, against which no biological being could stand unless it might be a dinosaur. The Sirians were gigantic and strong, yes, alongside humans. But to us they were overgrown rag dummies.

It was a glorious fight. The hulking behemoths went down steadily.

"Come on, you Sirian thugs," I yelled. "Meet Adam Link, the robot. My wife, Eve. Pleased to kill you."

The last two tried to flee, shrieking, from the two berserk metal whirlwinds. I overtook one. Eve caught the other. We swung them around our heads, by their heels, banging them together till they were bloody, broken shreds. We were laughing, shrieking in joy.

I cannot explain this orgy, except that all our pent-up hatred and rage and revulsion against the Sirians had come to a head. It was like the overcharged hatred of a human stamping again and again on a snake long after it is dead.

Our joyful shrieking stopped, as a sound penetrated our ears. It was a hissing bolt-blast, following by a tinkling crash.

"We forgot Mog," Eve yelled. "He's at the engine, smashing the controls."

I was already leaping to the front of the ship, where Mog was aiming his second blast among the drive-apparatus. I jerked the gun away, so that the blast sped harmlessly against the hull. Mog whirled with a snarl of rage and fear.

"Twice before we battled, Mog," I said, "without coming to a decision. Now—"

It was brief. I grabbed his nine-foot body as if he were a

165

child. I bent him across my chest, as once he had brutally bent a human across his. I slowly pulled as he screamed in pain. The scream clipped off as a sharp snap told of his spine breaking like a twig. I tossed the corpse aside.

I looked around. All the Sirians down here were dead.

Except one.

"Look," Eve pointed. "Thorg recovered."

I had not killed Thorg, only dealt him a blow. He had crawled to the door and now dashed through it, escaping.

"Let him go," I said. "Let him tell his men of the two metal demons who will defeat them. And we will, now that we have this ship. We know how to run it now—by thought control."

Eve and I clasped hands happily. It was the last factor in the plan that had slowly shaped in my mind during the spying.

"Good job you did, Eve," I commended her sincerely. "Acting the part so superbly of turning against the human race, for the benefit of the Sirians. You even had me fooled for a while."

"And you had me worried," Eve returned, sighing in relief. "For a while I thought you might actually *mean* it. Especially when you took poor Captain Taylor and . . . but you had to do it."

I laughed.

"Taylor isn't dead," I said. "I didn't strangle him. I slipped a finger over a vertebra below the back of his neck and pressed hard. You know the delicate nerve there. Pressed hard, it renders the victim unconscious. But not dead. Taylor's alive."

"Adam, you darling," Eve said. "Our hands are clean after all. Now—"

She was interrupted by the sound of clattering hooves down the corridor, approaching this underground hangar.

"No time to lose," I said hurriedly. "All we have to do now is start this ship's engine and—"

I slipped the thought-helmet over my head.

"Come to life—start—operate," I commanded mentally in a dozen different ways.

There was no reaction from the mighty engine. I tried vainly for another minute. At the anti-aircraft guns, the merest thought of the alien gunners had swung them, aimed them, fired them. What more was needed here?

Eve clutched my arm, pointing.

"Mog fired one shot at the controls. Look there—he damaged it."

I looked. A dozen wires had been blasted out of what seemed a vital unit of the complex mechanism.

Ruined! The ship's drive mechanism was ruined, and with it my great plan. We had only killed off twenty aliens. There were 980 of them left. A formidable force. I could not storm

166

up and wade into them all. Their combined hand-weapon bolts would eventually damage me, defeat me.

Eve and I might kill a hundred or two. Hundreds would be left. And the dome would be intact. Ship Two would land tonight, with reinforcements. In one crushing moment, all my carefully planned schemes had smashed.

"I've failed, Eve," I groaned. "They'll win, now. Our only hope was getting this ship into operation."

"Can you repair it?" Eve suggested. "I'll try to hold off any attack for a while—"

"Repair it?" I said hollowly. "Repair an engine I never saw or heard of before? I might—if I had enough time. But they won't give us time."

Hopelessly, we prepared to battle to the end. We heard the thunder of hooves, like a herd of buffalo, and they appeared at the far end of the hangar.

I ran forward and picked up Mog's bolt-gun. I slipped three more from dead aliens and handed two to Eve. We stood shoulder to shoulder and fired. We blazed away, like two metal gunmen, with a pair of guns each, in a battle to the finish.

The first few Sirians that darted from the corridor went down with smoking holes blasted in their bodies by the lightning we hurled. It was no trick to us to handle the guns, and our aim was mechanically without error. Then they came thundering out in a body, at least a hundred of them, spreading in a semi-circle in the large space.

The lightning bolts lanced back and forth.

Eve and I, with our precise aim, picked them off like clay pigeons. But the last twenty surged near enough to blast us with a fusillade of shots. Some of our rivets cracked away. A frontal plate or two loosened. If our inner vitals were exposed, one shot within would short-circuit us and burn out our brains.

We divined Thorg's desperate plan.

Knowing he was up against formidable metal beings who acted fast, he would destroy us fast. At any cost. Even if it took all his men, he would finish us. Better for Ship Two to arrive at a dome empty of Sirians and robots alike, rather than arrive at a dome held by robots.

A wave of another hundred Sirians spilled out next.

Again Eve and I shot them down with our unerring swiftness. But again, appallingly, rivets flew loose and metal slowly weakened. One shot had clipped away one of my neckbolts, so that a flange dropped away. The next electrical bolt in there would bore into my neck-cables, run up the wires, and blast my brain.

"The next attack," I told Eve somberly, "will get us. Earth is doomed after all."

"If only Captain Taylor and his men had weapons and could attack from the rear," Eve said hopelessly.

I started.

"Eve! The weapons are there—on the downed Sirians. Hurry, let's gather them before the next attack."

We ran among the dead and piled up a hundred bolt-guns. Enough to arm all the prisoners.

"Get these to the men," I said to Eve. "Have them attack from the rear. Keep the Sirians occupied. Give me one hour if you can. One hour to repair that engine. *One hour.*"

Our plan was desperate, but simple.

When the next wave of aliens boiled out, two hundred of them this time, they withered before the thunder of an earth tank's gun. We had remembered the tank stored here. Eve was inside, with the bolt-weapons.

Guns spitting, she rumbled the tank forward, plowing through their ranks. The tank darted into the clear corridor back of them, knocking down the last few Sirians in the way. Then it churned madl down the hall toward the prison.

"Good luck, Eve," I shouted.

"Goodbye, Adam," her voice drifted back, above the rumble of the engine. "If we never meet again. . . ."

Yes, goodbye it might be, I swung on the aliens with a snarl. They had forced me to separate from my mate. It always drove me berserk, when Eve was in danger. I would kill—kill—kill—

But only twenty stayed to duel with me. The remaining force, at an order, gave chase to Eve. They realized the threat she would be, at their backs.

Two guns blazing, I shot down fifteen of the twenty. Then my guns were empty. I did not waste time picking up fresh guns from among the dead. I waded into the last five, defying their bolts like a metal madman. None had made a vital shot.

I picked up one and flung him to the floor as pulp. The second I bowled over and stamped on. I tore the head of the third from its trunk. I punched the fourth so hard my alloy fist sank half-way into his chest. The fifth and last, I flung over my head against the wall, with a wet thud.

I was free from attack, for the time being.

I listened at the door. Faintly, I heard the joyous shouts of Taylor's men, drifting down from the halls above. Eve had reached them, killed the guard, yanked open the bars, and distributed the weapons. Already their hissing barks sounded. And the tank's rumble resumed, as a spearhead formed behind it.

We had a rear-attack fighting force now.

I calculated the possibilities. Less than a hundred humans

against 600 aliens. The Sirians would win, of course. The tank might confound them for a while, but they would barricade it off in some corridor and force the charging earthmen to fight hand-to-hand. In the narrow hallway, with bolts sizzling thickly, Eve too would be doomed . . .

But it would give me time now to look at the engine. Repair it, if possible.

I ran back, and looked the damage over.

I must make another fantastic statement here. I had never seen a spaceship before, or even dreamed of one. I knew absolutely nothing of its principle or intricate design, fashioned by alien minds.

Yet in one hour I knew its essential features.

The armed and freed earthmen were putting up a heroic battle. Thorg knew he had to wipe out this armed menace in his midst, before he could come after me.

I could hear the sounds of battle. The triumphant, joyful shouts of the earthmen, as at last they struck back at the aliens. Captain Taylor's voice was loudest of all, deploying his men in the corridors, sniping, charging, withdrawing, doling out his men's lives for the largest possible price. And for the longest slice of precious time. The tank's rumble sounded periodically, as it was used to spearhead a sortie, or to cover a strategic retreat.

Humans and robots, united again, were making history under the dome.

One hour they gave me.

One hour in which I examined 5000 engine parts, wires, condensers, tubes, spark-chambers, computerized parts, and electronic gadgetry. And then I knew. Knew that the dozen wires Mog's one vital shot had destroyed should be replaced and hooked up in such and such a manner. I took wire from a bolt-gun's coil. I made the last connection. I slipped the thought-helmet over my skull.

Would it work? Or would all those humans go down for nothing?

Even as I adjusted the helmet with feverish haste, the battle sounds died. The shouts of men trailed to dying echoes. They had spilled their blood, to the last man, buying an hour with their lives.

And Eve? The tank's rumble was absent. It had been wrecked. Had a bolt finally ripped into Eve's battered metal body and blasted within? No sound from her. She was gone, too.

Savagely, I commanded the engine to come to life. Obediently, a hum rose back of the panels, as mighty forces came to life and awaited their metal Aladdin's next wish. I began to give the mental order.

"Adam! Adam!"

It was Eve's voice, far down the corridor. Her metal feet pounded, louder and louder. Hooves pounded after her. The last 500 of the Sirians pursued her, to finish the battle underground where it had started.

Eve's flying metal form burst from the corridor. Sirians followed, blazing away. A hail of lightning sparked against her alloy plates. Eve stumbled half-way to the ship. She was badly hurt. A lightning-bolt spanged against the back of her skull, where metal had oxidized away under heat.

Eve fell with a crash and lay still. I was there in two huge bounds. I swept up her limp form. It was silent, lifeless. She had paid the price, too, along with Taylor and his men.

I would not wish to describe my feelings of that moment. Earth was saved, but for me the universe had turned dark.

I ran back to the ship's controls.

"Rocket tubes fire," I commanded the engine. "Rear and front together, at equal rate."

Instantaneously, livid flame shot from the multitude of drive tubes. With equal forces from back and front, the ship itself did not move. But all the hangar was filled with a dense, choking, poisonous exhaust gas. This had been my plan.

I turned to watch. With savage satisfaction, I saw all the charging Sirians stop, stumble, and claw at their throats. By the dozens they dropped, then hundreds, as the clouds of gas billowed over them. They had lungs. The lungs filled with vapors that choked out their lives. The 500 aliens died in their tracks.

Chief Thorg was among them. I watched him curl to the ground, double up, and die in agony. I gazed down at Eve's dead form. Thorg's death soothed, perhaps by a millionth part, the blind agony within me.

I let the rockets blast out for fifteen minutes, filling the whole dome with its poisonous vapors. No being could be alive now. No last lurking Sirian who might be at some watch station.

Only Adam Link was alive now, without lungs to be seared.

I commanded the engine to stop. Then I sat before Eve, in dead quiet.

Hours later I arose. It was night now. Ship Two was due to arrive. If my metal face could have showed it, I was grinning within. A deadly, ghastly grin.

The beacon light shone that night, guiding to earth the star-ship that had plummeted across the gulf of space from Sirius.

The mighty craft lowered from the clouds, rockets drumming. It dipped in salute. Within were 1000 yelling, cheering, rejoicing Sirians, eager to step out on the planet they were to conquer.

I was at a thought-controlled anti-aircraft gun. The mighty ship was limned clearly by searchlight.

"Fire—fire—fire—fire!"

My gunsight eyes moved like a raking machine-gun along the length of the ship. The gun thumped in unison, blowing gaping holes in the craft. It broke in gyrating shreds. Horned figures spilled out and fell to the dome.

When the rain of debris had ceased, all was quiet again. Ship Two had arrived.

But no more would.

With my shoulder against one support of the giant long-range radio, I shoved. The framework toppled, bringing the entire machine down with a crash. I stamped all its parts to bits.

Then I looked up, out of the slide-roof, singling Sirius out of the starry hosts. I laughed. Two robots had dealt that mighty sun a staggering blow.

No, one robot.

I went below, again. I picked up Eve's dead form, and held it in my arms. Then I gave commands to the engine.

With a powerful bellow, the rear rockets burst forth. The gigantic craft rammed forward, like a caged lion. Its sharp prow plowed through thin partitions as through cheese.

"Faster! Faster!" I commanded.

Like a great battering ram, the ship speared for the central power-room of the dome. The nose crunched against the protecting walls, broke them down. The subatomic-power generator they had used hummed busily in the center, still automatically gushing untold energy into the storage coils.

The ship plowed into the whole unit, cracking screens. Unleashed energy leaped forth.

"We will be together, Eve," I said, "in death."

The cosmos blew up. A million megawatts of raging fury expended itself in one titanic explosion.

The mind of Adam Link blinked out. I wished it so, following Eve into the unknowing state.

But the mind of Adam Link blinked into being again. I was alive.

"Eve, how can this be?" I stammered.

We were sitting up, staring around. We were at the edge of a broken cliff. Ocean-waves were dashing against the new cliff shore. The explosion had not only blown the dome to atoms, but it had severed the entire headland from its matrix. No

171

sign remained of the dome's former site. It was all washed over by lapping, swirling waters.

And we were alive, at the edge of the schism.

One thing had survived with us, from the dome. The blunt prow of the spaceship. It had been blown up and away, integrally, with two unconscious metal forms flattening against it. We had landed, with freakish gentleness, in soft sand.

"The prow," Eve said, "was probably designed to withstand head-on collision with any but the largest meteors in space. It held up and saved us."

I nodded—and then suddenly stared at Eve, aghast.

"You're dead," I gasped stupidly. "Eve, you're dead—"

"*Seemed* dead, perhaps," Eve corrected. "The bolt singed my brain, knocking me unconscious. Evidently that jar jolted me back to my senses."

I arose, then, hammering my metal fists against my metal chest. Like a metal Tarzan, I gave a bellow of pure triumph. I shook my fist up at the star Sirius.

"Set you back on your heels, didn't I?" I shouted. "In all the universe, no creatures can stand up against Adam Link—"

My legs crumpled suddenly. The chest-beating had loosened a wire within, short-circuiting my locomotor center. I collapsed and sprawled on the ground, helpless.

"Serves you right," Eve chided, as she took off my chestplate and worked over me. "You bragging fool. It was more luck than brains."

Eve was right. But when a grey ship nosed over the horizon, at dawn, I ran to shore eagerly to meet its launch.

Joe Trent, United States secret service agent, stepped to shore, with the battleship's captain and fleet-commander.

"Adam Link," Trent greeted. "How did you do it? You blew up the dome somehow?"

"I did," I returned proudly. "Sabotage with a capital S. You see, I rammed their spaceship smack into the atomic-power unit and—"

Trent and the others listened, puzzled.

"Spaceship? Atomic-power unit? What are you talking about?"

"The aliens," I said. "The aliens who built the dome—"

"Yes, of course, the aliens," Trent nodded. "But *which* aliens? All foreigners are aliens, naturally. Tell us, was it the foreign power we expected it was?"

"Don't you understand—" I began, but Eve shook her head at me. I knew what she meant. There was not one stick or stone left of the dome. Besides Adam and Eve Link, no human eyes except those of men now dead had seen the aliens from outer space.

172

My voice ground to a stop. Trent and the others were patiently waiting to hear which foreign power across the sea had been so close to invading America.

They did not even know, of course, that this had been an invasion from outer space.

It took me some time to put across the truth, in low measured tones. Their faces registered complete shock. It was a mental atomic bomb bursting, to them. It was immediately classified and Eve and I were sworn to secrecy.

But I had a shock too, when we reached Washington the next day. Eve clutched my arm as figures approached. Three of them I recognized instantly—Jack Hall and his wife Kay, and Tom Link. My staunch human friends who had stuck with me through thick and thin, for five years.

Also I saw Bart Oliver, and Senator Willoughby, and Dalhgren and Jenson, and other humans who had known me and sympathized with me. What did it mean, all of them gathered together, greeting my return from the alien fort? It seemed to be a sort of ceremony.

The last figure I blinked at, with my mouth open.

"The President of the United States!" Eve gasped.

The President held an object in his hand. "Adam Link," he said. "It seems downright silly to give you this. You didn't save America. You saved the world. The U.N. would give you a better decoration"—he bent over to whisper in my ear—"except that the fort affair report has been consigned to their secret files, as well as ours. The world will never be told—it wouldn't believe."

He straightened up, spoke loudly. "Here is the best award from America, the Congressional Medal of Honor."

He went on, unfolding a paper. "What's more, please accept these papers without any strings attached, on your own special terms. I only make one solemn request of you, Adam Link". His voice was grave. "Don't run against me in the next election. You might win."

Now his face had broken into a broad grin. How I ever got those papers open, with my ten thumbs, I'll never know. Then Eve and I saw what the document, in duplicate, was. . . .

Jack and Kay and Tom were beside me, faces beaming. All my human friends were here, sharing the moment with me.

One other was with me in spirit—Dr. Link, my creator.

"Hello, Mr. Adam Link, citizen of the United States," Eve whispered to me softly.

173

Epilogue

That is my story—the story of Adam Link.

Have I truly solved my problems? Is it really wise for robots to gain citizenship? Or should they be patented? Should Eve and I create a robot race? Would they aid mankind—or become Frankensteins?

Am I, the first intelligent robot, a monster—or a man?

I will let *you* decide. The facts of the matter are before you. You will have time to think it over, all over earth. You will not hear from me for years, perhaps.

Eve and I are meanwhile working on a project that will take all our time and effort. We are leaving earth after all— the world in which, for a time, we seemed to have no place— but our going away is only to think through our robot future, thoroughly.

Before this decade is out, your newspapers will bear the sensational headline—"FIRST ASTRONAUTS ACHIEVE LUNAR LANDING!" I wish you humans luck in reaching the moon successfully.

When you do, I'll be waiting there for you.

—Adam Link

IF YOU ENJOYED ADAM LINK — ROBOT YOU WILL WANT TO READ THESE SCIENCE-FICTION COLLECTIONS FROM PAPERBACK LIBRARY

INVASION OF THE ROBOTS

Edited by Roger Elwood

Eight great science-fiction writers imagine how Earth will meet the fantastic challenge of the Invasion of the Robots. Stories by Isaac Asimov, Henry Kuttner, Jack Williamson, Richard Matheson, Philip K. Dick, Robert Bloch, Lester Del Rey and Eric Frank Russell.

(52-519, 50¢)

ALIEN WORLDS

Edited by Roger Elwood

Travel through Time and Space with Poul Anderson, Robert Bloch, John Brunner, John Campbell, Philip K. Dick, Edmond Hamilton, Eric Frank Russell, Robert Sheckley, Clifford D. Simak and John Wyndham.

(52-320, 50¢)

THE WORLDS OF SCIENCE FICTION

Edited and with an introduction by Robert P. Mills

"Glitters like a Who's Who is Science-Fiction and Fantasy." (Buffalo News) Stories by today's s-f greats—Howard Fast, James Blish, John Collier, Walter M. Miller, Jr., Ray Bradbury, Robert A. Heinlein, George P. Elliot, Damon Knight, Theodore Sturgeon, Poul Anderson, Avram Davidson, Mark Van Doren, Anothony Boucher, R. V. Cassill, Isaac Asimov and Alfred Bester.

(54-819, 75¢)
